I0553532

this time around

Ellie Grace

This Time Around
Copyright © 2013, First Edition by Ellie Grace
Copyright © 2014, Revised Edition by Ellie Grace

All rights reserved.

No part of this publication may be reproduced or transmitted in any form
or by any means, electronic or mechanical, without express permission
from the author, except by a reviewer who may quote brief passages for
review purposes.

This book is a work of fiction. Names, characters, places, brands, media,
and incidents are either the products of the author's imagination or are
used fictitiously. Any resemblance to actual events, places or persons,
living or dead, is entirely coincidental.

Cover Design by Sarah Hansen of Okay Creations
Cover Photo by Julie Parker of Julie Parker Photography
Interior Formatting & Design by Stacey Blake, Hayson Publishing
Edited by Tawdra Kandle, Hayson Publishing

ISBN: 978-0-9914060-5-0

For all the amazing authors out there who inspired me to take a chance and share the story in my head.

chapter one

Nora

When I first set foot outside the airport and got a taste of the fresh South Carolina air, I felt like I could finally breathe again. Like I'd been holding my breath underwater and had finally reached the surface. I hadn't realized how much I'd missed being down here. Well... maybe I'd realized it, but I certainly hadn't let myself admit it. Over the last four years, I'd become pretty accustomed to pushing my feelings aside, especially my feelings about home. I'd managed to stay away for as long as I could, but now the time was right. Besides, it would only be for a little while.

I spent the two-hour drive with the windows down and the radio blaring in my rental car. Driving was one thing I had definitely missed. No one drove in New York City. Transportation consisted of flagging down cabs on the sidewalk or hopping onto the subway. Throw any kind of weather into the mix and forget it: be prepared to walk. After a few weeks in the city, and walking countless blocks in high heels, I'd learned to always carry flats in my purse.

Either way, no matter what form of transportation was used, it meant fighting the hordes of people, all of whom were also in a rush to get wherever they were going. That was another thing; city people are always in a hurry, always moving. There never seemed to be any time to just sit back and enjoy the ride before rushing on to the next thing. Perhaps that's why the last four years had gone by so fast.

In my hometown of Beaufort, South Carolina, things were completely different. It was a small southern town in the heart of Lowcountry, with a historic feel and the kind of scenic beauty that required people to slow down and enjoy it. Life seemed to move a little slower there, and I never truly realized it, or appreciated it, until I was thrown into the chaos of the city.

New York was beautiful in its own way, but to me, it paled in comparison to the natural magnificence of the south. The feel of the cool coastal breeze across your face, the quiet shade of the towering live oak trees, and swinging off a rope into the refreshing water of the river on a hot day; there was nothing quite like it, especially in the city. At heart, I was still just a small town girl.

Regardless, my time in the city wasn't over yet. At last week's graduation ceremony, I sat among the rest of my NYU classmates as we filled the endless sea of chairs, donning our violet caps and gowns, and baking under the hot sun as we waited to collect our diplomas. But, unlike many of my college peers who would be heading off to various parts of the country to begin the next chapter of their lives, my "higher education" chapter was still unfinished. When the summer was over, I would be heading back to NYU for my first semester of law school, and three more years of city living.

As I turned off the highway and crossed into Beaufort, all the comfort I'd felt when I first got off the plane vanished, and my stomach began twisting into knots. When I saw the oak trees draped with Spanish moss, the historic antebellum houses and the river lined with marsh, I was flooded with memories that made my heart ache. Now that I was actually here, it was easy to remember why I had fled to New York and stayed away for so long. Everything about this place made me think of him.

Jake.

I took a deep breath and attempted to calm myself down and

remind myself why I was here. My best friend Susie was getting married this summer, and as her maid of honor, I was determined to help her with the preparations and spend as much time with her as I could before the big day. I had also agreed to keep an eye on my father's law firm while he and my mother were away.

The reminder that my parents wouldn't be home gave me some relief. At least I would have some time to myself and wouldn't have to put on a show the second I walked through the door. They assumed that the only reason I hadn't been back all this time was because I was so busy with school and my summer internships, which was they'd been so understanding about all the missed holidays and having to come visit me in the city instead. They would never understand the real reason for my reluctance. After all, it had been four years. *Four damn years*! Frankly, I didn't really understand it myself. If someone told me that they'd avoided going home for that long after a breakup, I would probably have them sent in for a psych evaluation.

At least with my parents out of town, I would have a chance to get a grip on myself and figure out how to handle being here. Besides, I had no idea what Jake was doing, or if he was even in town anymore. I could deal with this. In a few short months, I would be leaving Beaufort behind. Again.

Pulling into my parents' driveway, I could see that not much had changed. The home I'd grown up in was exactly as I remembered it —white with dark blue plantation shutters and a two-story front porch that ran along the first and second levels— all of which was sitting beneath the tall oaks and magnolias. This had always been my haven, the one place I could always find peace. Now, even here I felt haunted. Still, it was good to be home.

I hauled my bags up the front steps and retrieved the spare key from its hiding place in the flower pot. After fiddling with the old lock for a few seconds, I swung open the front door and walked inside, pausing in the foyer to look around at the house I hadn't been in for so many years.

Aside from the redecorated living room and new pieces of artwork on the walls, it was mostly unchanged. I stepped into the den and inhaled the faint scent of cigar smoke that lingered in the air, even though my father had been away. The bookshelves were filled with the brown leather-bound law books that my father had inherited from his father before him, and the same elegant, clear glass bottles lined the bar, filled with pricey amber malts and whiskeys that my father sipped nearly every evening as he puffed on a cigar. Everything about this room reminded me of him, and I almost felt myself beginning to miss my parents. Almost.

I walked over to the old grand piano that sat in the corner and ran my fingers over the smooth wood, leaving a trail in the dust that had collected on it. I'd never once seen anyone play it, and I often wondered why my parents kept it there, sitting unused and wasting space. When I was younger, I'd tried to teach myself how to play, but it wasn't long before I realized that the piano just wasn't for me.

After a few minutes of wandering around my childhood home, I brought my bags upstairs to my bedroom. Walking in, it was as though no time had passed. It was completely untouched and exactly as I had left it all those years ago. I knew that my parents' house had more rooms than they could possibly need, but after being away so long, I still half-expected to find my stuff hauled out and replaced with gym equipment or some kind of "man cave". It was nice that they'd left it for me, as it was. I was reminded of how much they cared about me. I knew they had missed me, and for a split second I felt guilty for my feelings of relief about their absence.

Dropping my bags down, I swung open the French doors to the balcony for some fresh air before lying down on my bed to rest. As I studied the floral pattern of the duvet that I hadn't seen since I was a teenager, I felt my eyelids began to droop closed. All the traveling combined with my emotional turbulence had left me exhausted.

"Noraaaaaa!!!!"

I awoke with a start when I heard a voice outside. I glanced out the window at the changing color of the sky as dusk began to fall.

"Nora Montgomery! Get down here now!"

Standing up groggily, I walked out to the balcony and looked below to see the familiar blonde hair and cheery smile of my best friend, Susie.

"SUSIE! What are you doing here?" I yelled down to her.

"Here to see my best friend, duh."

"Don't move I'll be right down," I said as I rushed back out through my bedroom and down the stairs to meet her.

Opening the front door, I greeted Susie with a big hug. "I thought you weren't coming back until tomorrow?" I asked her as we walked through the house into the kitchen.

"Ethan and I finished our packing early so we got in yesterday," she answered. "How does it feel to be home? I really cannot believe it's been so long since you've been back!"

"Yeah, it's been a long time." I went to the fridge and grabbed a bottle of white wine. "I've really missed it here," I told her truthfully as I poured two glasses.

We sipped our wine and caught up on everything from the few months since we'd last seen each other. Even though I hadn't been home since I left for school in New York, Susie and I always made time to spend together. She would visit me in New York, or I would make the trip to Virginia where she and her boyfriend Ethan (now her fiancé), had gone to school at the University of Virginia. We'd all been close growing up. Susie and I had been inseparable since the age of four, and Ethan and Jake grew up next door to each other. When Susie and Ethan got together in high school, it wasn't too long before Jake and I started seeing each other, too. After that, we did just about everything together.

"Well, I have to get home to have dinner with my parents," Susie said as she stood up. "But you and I are going out tonight. No excuses!"

"Okay," I laughed. "But wouldn't you and Ethan rather have some alone time?"

"No way!" she said. "I think we can handle a night apart. Besides, he's already going out tonight with, uh… his friend."

I smiled at her attempt of a cover-up. As though I didn't know which "friend" she was talking about. Susie was good about not mentioning Jake. I had made it pretty clear that I didn't want to talk about him, and over the years she had stopped trying to bring him up in conversation. I was grateful for that. However, her little slip-up did reveal that Jake was still here in town and hadn't moved away like I'd wished. Beaufort was a small town, and my stomach dropped at the mere idea of running into him. I'd known I would have to see him at the wedding–he was Ethan's best friend–but I'd hoped that I would have some time to mentally prepare before then.

"I'll pick you up at 8:30!" Susie yelled out her car window as she began pulling out of the driveway. "Wear something sexy!"

Jake

I took a step back to get a better look at my work. It wasn't much, but it was getting there.

Over the last few months, I'd started to work on renovating my grandfather's fishing cabin. Well, it was more like a shack right now, but it wouldn't be when I was done with it. It had been falling down for years, and my parents had finally given me the go-ahead to work on it. I'd always loved this place. Even though the building was battered and run-down, it was tucked away in the woods and sat right on the lake with a little dock for swimming and fishing.

Throughout my entire childhood and teenage years, I'd spent a lot of time in this place. But, as much as I'd enjoyed being here, I stopped coming a few years ago and hadn't been back until I started the renovation. When Ethan announced that he and Susie were getting married, I decided to finally fix this place up so I could let them use it. We had all spent a lot of time at the cabin back then, and I knew how much they loved it. This place held a lot of memories. Memories that still made my throat tighten and my chest ache, even after four years.

I met Nora during the spring of my senior year of high school, shortly after Ethan and Susie got together. Nora and Susie were a year behind us in school, so even though I'd seen her around, I didn't know much about her. All I really knew was that she was a Montgomery–rich, smart, privileged–definitely not the type of girl that would hang around a "bad boy" like Jake Harris. Not that I'd ever done anything really bad, just stupid teenage-boy crap. But it was a small town, and when someone was labeled a bad seed, it stuck, and everyone had a tendency to believe it.

When Ethan first tried to get Nora and me together, I had scoffed and told him he was crazy. *"Why would I want to get with a snob like that?"* I'd said. As much as I loved Ethan, I wasn't going to pretend to be interested in some random girl just so we could all hang out together. Not my style. Especially not when there were a shit load of other girls I could be giving my attention to. Ones who were much more my speed. Why have just one girl when you could have lots of girls? That was my philosophy.

Then, one especially hot day in April, Ethan and I decided to go up to the fishing cabin. We were hanging out on the dock, drinking beers, when he told me that he'd invited Susie and Nora. Before I had time to protest, I saw them coming out of the woods and heading our way. Ethan ran over to Susie, but Nora just kept walking toward me. Without saying a word, she pulled her tank top over her head and shimmied out of her cutoff denim shorts, revealing a tiny black bikini underneath. She walked past me to the edge of the dock, dove right into the water, surfaced, and swam back over before gracefully climbing out. I'd been watching her since she arrived, and as she spread out her towel and sat down, I couldn't take my eyes off her. She glistened in the sun as beads of water slid down her tan skin, her rich brown hair falling down her back and clinging to her perfect body.

She was the most beautiful thing I'd ever seen.

When her hazel eyes finally met mine, she flashed me a grin and said, *"So, Jake Harris… are you just gonna sit there and stare, or are you gonna offer me a beer?"*

I couldn't help but smile as I remembered it.

From that moment on, I was totally hooked. I'd known she was different. Nothing like I'd assumed, but still unlike any girl I'd ever met. Within minutes, I'd grabbed my phone to text whichever girl I had plans with that night and cancel. I didn't make any more plans after that, and I stopped noticing other girls altogether.

Until that point, I'd never really pursued a girl before. At least, not for anything more than a couple dates or a hookup. I'd had no idea what I was doing. All I knew was that I wanted to be around her. I wanted to know her.

Unfortunately, I had no clue how to go about it. The girls I was used to were easy… in every sense of the word. Nora was different. She didn't hang all over me, making up excuses to touch me any chance she got, or bat her eyelashes and laugh at everything I said, even when it wasn't remotely funny. Instead, she called me on my bullshit, teased me when I deserved it, and didn't flinch about getting a little dirt under her fingernails. She challenged me. And I loved it.

I had resorted to tagging along with Ethan and Susie like a pathetic third-wheel any time I thought she might be with them. I could tell she didn't take me seriously, not that I could really blame her. I'd dated or messed around with half the girls in town and had never been with one person for longer than a week or two. I knew that I would have to do something to make her realize that I wasn't just messing around with her, and in order to do that I needed to spend some time alone with her.

Since she never would have agreed to go out with just me, I had to beg Ethan and Susie to help me out. After making fun of me for quite a while–*"Jake Harris needs help getting a date? Oh how the mighty have fallen!"* –they finally agreed to make plans with Nora for all of us to hang out at the cabin. Of course, Ethan and Susie had no intention of actually showing up there, which would give me a chance to finally be alone with Nora.

The day of our "date" finally arrived, and everything at the cabin was set up perfectly. I'd planned everything out and spent most of the day getting ready. Twinkle lights were strung up along the path to the water and down the dock, and music played from an old radio that I'd found in my dad's garage. There was supposed to be some kind of meteor shower that night, so I'd brought blankets and set up lawn chairs so we could watch it. I didn't know shit about romance, but I thought I'd done pretty damn good.

When Nora walked down to the dock, I'd handed her the flowers that I'd picked from my mom's garden. I could still remember the look on her face. I'd never seen anyone look so confused, but there was a hint of excitement in her eyes when she began to realize what was going on.

Moving in real close, I'd looked down at her and said, *"So, Nora Montgomery... are you just gonna stare at me, or are you gonna give me a chance?"*

By some miracle, she had actually decided to stay, and we sat down at the end of the dock with the radio on, staring up at the sky as I took her hand and entwined my fingers with hers. I don't remember anything about what was going on in the sky that night, but I didn't care. I barely took my eyes off her. At some point she'd turned to me, and our eyes met. Without saying a word I'd leaned over and kissed her. After that, we'd been inseparable.

Just thinking about it made my chest constrict, filling me with agony. So I pushed the memories aside and started packing up my tools. Ethan was meeting me at my apartment in an hour, and I was in desperate need of a shower. A night out would be good for me. I'd been so busy with work and classes over the last few months that I barely ever left the house unless it was to go to a construction job or a class on campus. Now that I was finally finished with school, I couldn't wait to unwind a little bit.

Ethan and I went down to the waterfront to grab some food. As we sat in the booth waiting for it to come, he held his beer up.

"Here's to you, Mr. Architect," he said. "I never thought I'd see the day."

"That makes two of us," I chuckled. "And here's to the future groom."

"Hear, hear!"

We clinked our beers together. It was strange to think about how much we'd grown up. Ethan had been my best friend for as long as I could remember, and it seemed like just yesterday we were stealing beer from the neighbors and getting in brawls with the idiots at school. Despite how much had changed, sometimes I felt like I was permanently stuck at the age of eighteen.

Ethan, on the other hand, was gearing up to marry his high school sweetheart, and he couldn't have been happier. After we graduated from high school, he had taken a year off to stay in town while Susie finished her senior year. Then they'd both gone off to college together; somehow managing to beat the odds and stay true to one another. Ethan had proposed to her over their Christmas vacation, and frankly, I was surprised he'd managed to wait that long. He'd wanted to put a ring on her finger for almost as long as he'd known her.

In a lot of ways, I envied what they had together. It seemed so stable and uncomplicated. Sure, they'd faced their struggles throughout the years, but they'd continually managed to come out stronger on the other side. For them, love had always been enough. If only it were that simple for everyone.

"So, what's next?" Ethan asked. "Are you thinking about joining a firm, or are you gonna work on your own?"

"Still figuring it out," I said. "There aren't many architectural firms nearby, so it would mean branching out. I'd love to work on my own, but I've gotta get some projects under my belt first, and even then, who knows if I could actually generate any business here. You know how people are in this town ... So, for now I'm still working with my dad, and maybe soon I'll get some projects going."

My dad worked in construction, and since I'd been working with him on jobs for as long as I could remember, I already knew a lot of contractors and architects in the area. Unfortunately, Beaufort was a small town, and most people here still saw me as the troublemaker I'd been when I was growing up. Especially the wealthy folks. If I were smart, I would get out of here and start fresh someplace else, but I couldn't bring myself to do it. Not yet anyway. I felt like I was tied to this place, and I couldn't really understand why.

"How's the wedding stuff going?" I asked, changing the subject. "Has Susie turned into bridezilla yet?"

"Not yet, but she's been so preoccupied with final exams and moving back down here that she hasn't had time to start freaking out. Now that we're here, and she's giving it her full attention, I'll probably have to run for cover eventually."

After we ate, Ethan and I walked down Bay Street to find a place to settle in and grab a few drinks. When we passed one of the local favorites, The Landing Bar, we saw that a familiar band was playing, so we decided to check it out. I was two steps from the door when I heard the gentle strumming of a guitar, followed by a voice that halted me in my tracks. I'd recognize her voice anywhere.

Nora was sitting on a stool on the makeshift stage, strumming the guitar as she sang "Wagon Wheel." The girl loved to sing, and I loved listening to her sing. So much of our time together had been spent with her singing and playing guitar while I just laid back and enjoyed it. I'd always told her that she had the most beautiful voice I'd ever heard. She still did.

Cowering behind the other people standing in the bar, I kept my head low and watched her. She looked exactly the same and still made my mouth water. She was wearing a short pink lacy dress with her brown cowboy boots. Her long brown hair came down in light waves, and her eyes sparkled. She lit up the entire room. When Nora was around, it was impossible to notice anyone but her.

I couldn't believe she was here. Being near her made me ache with longing. Even though I'd expected her to be in town for the wedding, I didn't think she arrive so soon... and nothing could have prepared me for seeing her now.

chapter two

Nora

When I was in high school, I'd sung with the band that was playing at The Landing, but I couldn't believe they had actually pulled me up on stage with them. Normally, I would try to talk my way out of it, but my confidence was fueled by the shots of vodka that Susie had pushed at me earlier in the evening. She had also begged me to do it "as an engagement present." I had a sneaking suspicion that there were going to be a lot more "favors" before this wedding was over. Fortunately, I loved Susie like a sister, so I would do just about anything for her.

There was a time when I would have eagerly jumped up on stage with the band, but the truth was I had barely sung or even picked up my guitar since moving to New York. I was okay without singing; but what did bother me was that I hadn't written a single song or even a lyric in the past four years. I'd been writing songs for as long as I could remember. It had started off as just a few lyrics here and there, but by the time I entered high school, I had notebooks full of the songs that I'd written. Part of the reason I'd agreed to go to New York for school was so that I might be able to pass my songs along to someone in the music industry. That didn't happen. I never even tried.

My best songs were the ones written during the time I was

with Jake. He had incited feelings in me that I'd never experienced before and hadn't experienced since. Putting those feelings on paper had helped me to understand them better, but after he broke my heart, I just didn't feel inspired to write anymore.

Periodically over my first few months in the city, I had tried to sit down and write a song about what happened. I'd never written a "breakup" song before, but there were plenty of them out there. I thought it might help me move on if I could put it into lyrics with a melody, but how could I when I didn't even understand what had happened? My head and my heart were full of questions that I didn't have the answers to, and it was too painful for me to sift through the memories and relive it over and over again. Eventually I stopped trying.

As nervous as I was to be on stage again, I managed to make it through the song I was singing with only a few off-pitch moments. It was a miracle, considering how anxious I was and how long it had been since my last attempt at singing. When it was over, I stepped off the small stage and awkwardly accepted praise from a few people on my way over to the bar where Susie was standing. As I leaned across the bar to order another drink, I heard an all-too-familiar voice behind me.

"You are amazing."

I closed my eyes and took a deep breath before turning around to face him.

"Hello Jake." I kept my voice as even as possible, trying to ignore the tingle climbing up my spine and the knots forming in my stomach.

His mouth tilted in a half smile. "Welcome home, Nora. How have you been?"

"What are you doing here?" I asked, ignoring his question. I didn't understand how he could appear so calm while I was barely managing to hold it together. So many emotions were surging through me that I wasn't sure how to act. It didn't help that he still made me weak in the knees, and the fact that he had that affect on me, despite what he'd done, only made me angrier.

"I'm here with Ethan," he said, shifting uncomfortably. "Is that a problem for you?"

"Of course not, you can do whatever you want. You always did anyway, right?" I was acting like a brat, but I couldn't help it. It still hurt, and the alcohol had removed any verbal filter I might have had.

"I guess I deserved that." He winced slightly. "Can I tell you how good you look, or are you going to yell at me for that, too?"

He still had the same easygoing charm and irresistible grin, but I could detect a sadness hidden beneath the surface that I'd never seen there before. I decided to ease up a little bit and try not to act like such a jerk.

"Thanks," I said. "You don't look too bad yourself." He looked *too* good, and I really wished he didn't. He hadn't changed much since the last time I'd seen him, aside from filling out a little more, which only added to his already-gorgeous appearance. He wore jeans and an old t-shirt that clung to his chest and arms, showing off his lean, well-toned frame. His dark blond hair fell softly over his forehead, and his eyes… those deep blue eyes that had always mesmerized me… looked into mine with a keen familiarity that sent shivers through my body.

"Your folks must be glad you're home," he commented, inching a little bit closer to me.

"Yeah, but they're actually away right now." I attempted to move back from him and put some distance between us, but my back was already pressed up against the bar. I couldn't think clearly when I was this close to him. It felt like there was an electric current running between us, drawing me to him while simultaneously turning my brain into mush.

"I've missed you, Nor." He reached for my hand and gave it a gentle squeeze. "I'm glad you're back."

I couldn't help the blush that rose to my cheeks when I felt his skin on mine. I'd always loved the feel of his rough, strong hands, and it brought me back to a place that I'd been desperately trying to avoid.

"Can I take you out for dinner or a drink sometime? To catch up?" he asked.

His words pulled me out of the haze I was in, and I yanked my hand away from his.

"Why bother?" I snapped. "The last time we made plans you never bothered to show up." Had he somehow forgotten what had happened between us, or did he just not care? How could he act so casual after what he'd done to me? My eyes were welling up with tears that I tried to blink away before he saw. I hated him for making me feel this way, and for acting like everything was the same between us. It wasn't the same, and it never would be again. How could he not realize how much he'd hurt me back then?

"That was a long time ago," Jake said softly, shifting his eyes to the floor. "And you left before I even had a chance to explain."

"No explanation necessary," I replied, straightening myself up. I wouldn't let him see how much it still upset me after all this time. "It doesn't matter anymore. Things have changed."

"I know."

The hurt was evident on his face, but I didn't let it get to me this time. He was the one who had hurt *me*. This was his own fault, and if he was offended, then too bad. I couldn't pretend like everything was fine and normal between us, and that we could carry on as if nothing had happened.

"I should get going." I brushed past him before he had a chance to stop me. I needed to get out of there and clear my head. Susie stopped me before I reached the door. She'd seen me talking to him so I didn't need to explain why I was leaving.

"You should give him a chance, Nora," Susie said. "Maybe there's more to the story than you think."

Her words took me by surprise. She'd never said anything like that to me before. What could she possibly mean by that?

"It doesn't matter," I replied casually. "It was a lifetime ago, right?"

"If you say so. I was going to get a ride home with Ethan, but do you want me to go with you?"

"No, it's fine," I told her. "I could really use some fresh air." It was only a ten minute walk back to my house, and it was a clear, bright night. I needed the walk. I was a complete mess. My head was flooded with all the memories that I'd been trying so hard to shut out. Unfortunately, I could remember it all like it was yesterday…

Jake and I had been together for almost a year. Which, in high school, was a really long time. He'd come into my life so unexpectedly, bringing color to my otherwise gray world, and wound up being completely different than I'd expected. He'd gone out of his way to prove to me that his days of serial hookups with the never-ending supply of girls were over. Once we had gotten together, he'd never so much as glanced at anyone else. He treated me like I walked on water. We spent nearly every waking moment together, but somehow it had never been enough, and we never got bored with one another. Each kiss thrilled me as much as the first one had, and every touch left me hungry for more.

He'd graduated a year before me, but since he hadn't had plans for college, we didn't have to worry about being apart from each other during my senior year. Our relationship went on without missing a beat. Jake worked with his dad during the day and hung out with me at night. When my parents lectured me about devoting all my time to him and forbade me from going out, he would sneak into my bedroom window once they'd fallen asleep. It was a rare occasion that we would actually spend twenty-four hours apart. However, when my own graduation passed and the weeks of summer started slipping away, we knew that a big change was coming.

My college applications had been planned out long before Jake and I got together, and my parents had been very specific about which schools were acceptable. None of them were close to home. My father was determined to have me follow in his footsteps and attend NYU, his alma mater. At that point in time, I'd been pretty dead-set on experiencing a new life outside of Beaufort, so I'd gone along with it. Of course, once Jake and I were together, I'd hated the idea of being so far away, but my parents wouldn't budge. I tried to sneak an additional application in the mail to a college in state, but when my father managed to intercept it, he lectured me like I was a child.

"Do you have any idea how stupid and immature it is to change your plans for some boy that you barely know? For a relationship that won't last? This is your future! You're better than this, Nora." I was aware that my parents weren't particularly fond of Jake, but they knew how I felt about him. I could get my degree anywhere. That argument was the first time I'd ever really clashed with my parents. Before that, I had always gone along with their plans for me like the dutiful daughter they expected me to be.

Naturally I was disappointed to have to go so far away, but Jake had promised that we would make it work, and we tried not to let it ruin our time together. I would be home for Thanksgiving and vacations, and he promised to visit me in New York City. I'd even started making plans to transfer to a college that was closer to home at the end of the semester. I'd hoped that by then my parents would see that it wasn't some childish "fling" between Jake and me and finally begin letting me make my own decisions.

As crazy as Jake and I were for each other, our relationship had always been pretty innocent. I mean, we kissed each other senseless, and there was definitely a lot of groping in the back of his pickup truck, but we'd never gone all the way. I'd wanted to, but Jake had been surprisingly resistant. He'd been with plenty of girls before me, but he always told me that it was different with me. He didn't want to mess things up by rushing into sex.

When summer came to an end and my remaining time in Beaufort went from weeks to days, Jake and I finally made plans to take that next step. We loved each other, and I wanted to experience everything with him. He was going to pick me up at home, and we were going to go to the fishing cabin where we'd met and where we'd spent so much of our time together. It was going to be perfect.

I'd been so excited that day. I got myself ready from head to toe, and bought the most beautiful lace bra and panties that I wore under my sundress. I'd been so excited for Jake to see.

When it was finally time for our date I'd gone out to sit on the front porch to wait for him, but he hadn't shown up. After an hour, I'd driven out to the cabin in case I'd gotten mixed up and was supposed to meet him there, but it was dark and he was nowhere to be found. He didn't answer his phone, which never happened when I called, and when I drove by his house, his truck wasn't there.

I'd been so confused. I couldn't understand what was going on. I'd always known that Jake could have just about any girl he wanted, and he'd obviously decided that it wasn't worth it to have one that was going to be thousands of miles away. Not to mention that I was totally inexperienced. Guys like Jake didn't want a girl who had no idea what she was doing. Even though he'd told me he loved me and promised to make it work, he'd clearly had a change of heart. That had been his way of ending it.

I didn't have any other explanation. Jake had told me once that he never actually broke up with any of the girls that he "dated"; instead he just stopped calling and ignored them until they got the hint that he was done with them. He always told me that I was "special," so I never considered that he would do that to me. Apparently, I was wrong. About everything.

I'd cried that whole night. Part of me had still hung on to the notion that he loved me and that the whole thing had to be a mistake. I'd expected him to call me or show up on my doorstep to apologize, but he never did. That was when I knew it was really over.

After convincing my parents to let me leave for school in New York a couple days early, I was gone. Once I got there, I'd changed my number and refused to speak to anyone about him. I hated him for what he'd done to me and for turning me into a shell of the person that I used to be.

What more could there possibly be to the story? Did it even matter anymore? Whatever Susie knew, or thought that she knew, she was obviously just confused or seriously misinformed. He'd abandoned me. It was as simple as that. He made me fall in love with him, and then he'd broken me. I wasn't the same after that.

As I walked home from the bar and remembered that day, I couldn't help the tears that broke free and cascaded down my cheeks. It had been a long time since I allowed myself to relive those memories, and the pain still cut me just as deep as it did on the day that it happened.

When I got back to my house, I went straight up to my bathroom and splashed cold water on my tear-stricken face. Being around Jake was something I would have to get used to if I was going to be here all summer, and since I refused to break down and cry every time I saw him, I knew that I had to find a better way to deal. As I changed into a comfy shirt to sleep in, I made a silent vow to myself that from this point forward, I would keep it together. I would be polite and friendly whenever I encountered him, but my walls would stay up, and I wouldn't let him see me get emotional. I would never shed another tear for Jake Harris.

Satisfied with my new resolve, I curled up in bed under the covers and waited for sleep to come.

Jake

When I woke up the next morning, the sun was pouring in the windows and my head felt like it was going to split in two. After Nora had run off on me the night before, I'd stayed at the bar and downed a few too many shots of whiskey. More than once I'd considered going after her, but Susie insisted that Nora needed some time.

"She just got home Jake," Susie had told me the night before. "She's been gone for a long time and it's a lot to take in. It's going to take her a little while to get used to being back here and face the past she left behind, but she'll come around."

I wasn't entirely sure that Susie was right about that. Nora seemed to really hate me. I thought she was finally starting to warm up to me, until I tried to make plans with her, and she stormed off.

It surprised me that she was still so angry, but I couldn't blame her if she hated me forever. What I'd done to her four years ago was unforgivable, and it was not like she could get inside my head and understand the reason why I'd done what I did. The only person who knew the truth was Ethan, and he had probably told Susie at some point because they both kept pressing me to explain it to Nora. Although that seemed like the easy answer, I knew it was more complicated than that. Sure, it might be the only way that she would ever forgive me, but it also might end up hurting her even more, and I couldn't bear to do that. It involved more than just me. Even though I believed that Nora should know the truth, it should come from someone else.

On the other hand, what did it mean that Nora was still so angry? If she'd moved on after all this time, would she still be so upset?

The idea that Nora might be holding onto any feelings for me was enough to get me out of bed. It was a long shot, but if there was any chance at all that she might still care, I had to at least explore it. I'd never really considered the possibility– heck, until last night I didn't even realize it was something I wanted. Seeing her had brought everything back to the surface, and if I were going to sort through all these feelings and figure out what they meant, I was going to have to spend more time with her. If only she would let me.

My dad needed some help at a job near town, so I threw on my work clothes and headed out to my truck. Before I could get in I heard barking from the porch, where my yellow lab, Max, was anxiously waiting for me to take him with me.

I gave in and lowered the tailgate. "Okay, c'mon, boy!" He happily jumped up into the back of the truck and sat down. Max almost always came with me to job sites. He was well behaved and usually just curled up in the shade and kept an eye on me. Besides, the construction guys loved him.

Glancing down at the address my dad had given me, I couldn't help but chuckle when I saw that the job we were working on was right near Nora's house. It was as if the universe was trying to push us together.

I slowed down as I passed her house and snuck a peek down the driveway, but there was no sign of her. I'm not sure what I was expecting to see. It wasn't like she would be standing out there waiting for me, and yet I longed to catch even a glimpse of her.

When I reached the house we were working on, I pulled into the driveway and did my best to put all thoughts of Nora aside so I could get to work.

When the work day was finally over I took Max out to the clearing behind the house to throw a stick for him and let him run around a little bit. I loved this area. It was quiet, secluded, and backed up to the river. Certainly not the kind of place I would ever be able to afford, even if I did manage to make it as an architect, and right now the idea of making it as an architect seemed like an abstract idea. It wasn't that I didn't like working construction. I actually enjoyed it. I liked the hard work, and it kept me in shape. The thing

I couldn't stand was constructing *someone else's* designs. I was constantly picking things apart in my head and thinking of all the ways that I would do it differently. I knew that I could be better than most of the architects I'd worked with in the past, I just needed a chance to prove it. All I wanted was to be able to use my ideas to create a design, and then see it through until the end. Unlike most of the architects I knew, I wasn't the type who would simply provide the plans and then move on to the next project; I would be there from start to finish.

My thoughts were interrupted when I saw Max stop, perk his ears up, and then take off running in the opposite direction of where I was standing.

"Hey, Max! Get back here!" I yelled, running after him through the clearing and into the trees. "Come here, boy!"

I chased him until I reached a very familiar backyard where he had finally stopped at the edge of the poolside patio. The universe was definitely working overtime today.

"Well, aren't you a sight for sore eyes?" I grinned.

Nora looked up from where she was crouched next to Max, gently stroking his fur and scratching behind his ears. "I take it this guy belongs to you?" she said, standing up. "What's his name?"

I had to take a minute to collect myself before answering because, so help me God, she was wearing the hottest little white bikini I'd ever seen, and every perfect curve was on display. She was still mouthwatering.

"This is Max," I responded, trying not to stare. "Sorry about this, I was just finishing up a job across the field when he took off on me. Apparently my dog has good taste in women."

Nora laughed, pretending not to notice the fact that I was gawking at her like an idiot. She seemed to hate me less today, so maybe Susie was right about her needing more time to settle in. I hated seeing her upset, and I couldn't stand it if she hated me forever.

"Are you still working with your dad?" she asked.

"For now, I am. But I actually just got my degree in architecture, so I'm trying to get started with that. It will probably take a 'lil while."

"Wow, that's really great. Good for you, Jake. I always knew you had it in you."

"Yeah, I know you did," I replied wistfully. "Thank you, and congrats to you, for graduating. Let me guess, top of your class?"

"Not exactly," she laughed. "I did okay, though."

"Of course you did. You always were the brains of the group. You could do anything you set your mind to."

For a split second, I saw a familiar look in her eyes, the one that I used to see when she still loved me, but then it was gone.

We stood there in silence for a few minutes, neither of us sure what to say. As much as I wanted to stay there with her, I figured I should probably leave on a good note. Since she actually seemed open to spending time with me, I didn't want to ruin it by saying something stupid.

"I should probably get going. Sorry, again, for the intrusion. Although... not that sorry," I winked, turning to walk away.

"Hey, Jake?" she called after me.

I turned around. "Yeah?"

"I was thinking about throwing a little engagement party for Susie and Ethan here at the house before my parents get back into town. What do you think?"

"Sounds like a great idea," I said. "I'd love to help out, if you'll let me."

"That would be great, if you don't mind," she said with a tentative smile. "I'm sure I'll need all the help I can get."

We made plans to get together the following day, and then Max and I started the walk back to my truck. I tried not to get my hopes up; it wasn't as though we had a date or anything, I was just helping her plan a party. Even so, the idea of spending time with Nora had me practically floating on a cloud the whole way home. All I could think about was that look in her eyes that I'd been missing for way too long.

chapter three

Nora

I tried to ignore the excitement pulsing through my veins on the day that Jake was coming over to help me with the party. Even though I'd told myself to stay away from him as much as possible, I'd decided to stop over-thinking things and just go with it. Jake and I could be friends. In fact, with our two best friends getting married, it was the only logical option.

Just friends, I reminded myself. It didn't matter that he made my heart race when he touched me, or that I got butterflies when I looked into his deep blue eyes. Old habits died hard, right? And the excitement I was feeling was just excitement for the party. That was it.

Before Jake was due to arrive, I had to stop by my father's law firm. He'd called the day before to let me know that he'd planned for someone to show me around and introduce me to all the associates. Not exactly my ideal morning, but I knew better than to argue with him about it.

I pulled into the small lot next to the sign that read *Montgomery & Partners*, and parked the car. My dad had big plans to rename the firm "Montgomery & Montgomery" when I graduated from law school. All part of his master plan. Sometimes I felt like nothing more than a piece in his puzzle, but I'd stopped trying to fight him on everything. He might deny it, but I knew that he'd always wanted to have a son who would follow in his footsteps. However, I was all he got. Sometimes I wished that I had a brother to take some of the heat off me, and then maybe I'd have a chance to do what I really wanted to do. Whatever that might be.

When I walked in the front entrance, I was met by a young guy, tall with dark hair, clean-shaven, and wearing a fancy suit. He couldn't have been much older than me.

"Hey there," he greeted me. "You must be Nora. Your father's told me a lot about you. I'm Carter Townes, one of the new junior associates."

"It's nice to meet you," I said, shaking his outstretched hand.

He led me inside, steering me toward the back offices. "Your dad mentioned that you're here for Ethan and Susie's wedding. I'm good friends with Ethan's older brother, so I'll be there, too."

"That's great. I'm sure it will be a lot of fun." I thought he'd looked familiar. "I'm actually planning a little engagement party for them on Friday at my parent's house. You should come by if you can."

"I'd love to. I'll be there," he replied with a grin. "Now, what do you say I go over what you're going to be helping us out with while you're here?"

Carter showed me around the firm, all the while regaling me with stories from his time at law school and telling me how well I would do there. Clearly another part of my father's strategy to keep me on track. My dad was so obvious sometimes. I really couldn't blame poor Carter for following orders, so I did my best to seem excited about the whole thing and smile politely while he made small talk.

As I left the office, I thought about what it might be like to be with someone like Carter. He was certainly the kind of guy who *should* get me excited. He was successful, driven, good looking–and obviously someone who my father would approve of–but I just didn't feel it. I'd faced the same problem when I was at school. I'd never met anyone who gave me that nervous, excited feeling that goes along with being really attracted to someone. Perhaps I'd never given anyone enough of a chance. Not all relationships were love at first sight. What if I'd been missing out on great opportunities all this time?

When I got back to the house, I changed out of my professional-looking slacks and blazer and threw on some denim shorts and a white t-shirt before Jake arrived. I searched through the basement for the decorations that my parents kept stored away for all the cocktail parties and law firm get-togethers that they were constantly throwing. Of course, they were exactly where my mom had told me they would be, neatly packed in plastic boxes with labels on the outside in my mom's perfect handwriting. Nothing in the Montgomery house was ever out of place.

I'd already called both Susie and Ethan's parents about the party, and they had agreed to spread the word to family and friends. Since it was so last minute, we decided to keep it simple, serving food cooked on the grill and setting up a small bar where people could make their own drinks.

Jake pulled into the driveway. I watched through the window as he hopped out of his old pickup truck and climbed the steps to the front porch. He paused in front of the door, shifting nervously on his feet before finally knocking, and then stepped back to wait for me to let him in.

After double-checking my appearance in the hallway mirror, I opened the door for him. His eyes automatically traveled down my body, taking me in from head to toe. I tried to hide the pleased blush that rose to my cheeks and threatened to give me away.

"Come on in," I greeted him. "Are you ready to be put to

work?"

His eyes snapped up and met mine. "Absolutely. I'm all yours."

Jake carried the boxes of decorations out back to the patio, and I began digging through them in search of anything that we could use. I pulled out a few strings of lights and some big round paper lanterns and laid them all out.

"I was thinking we could string the lights up around the patio," I said. "What do you think?"

"Sounds good to me," he said. "Just tell me what you need me to do."

"I'm going to go find a ladder so we can hang these, I'll be right back."

"Nah, you don't need a ladder, just hold on tight," he said with a smirk. Before I had a chance to protest, he was crouching down and hoisting me up onto his shoulders.

"Jake!" I squealed. "What are you doing? You're going to drop me!"

"Don't worry, I gotcha. I came here to help, didn't I? Besides, there are definite benefits to this method." He squeezed my thighs where he was holding onto me.

His warm touch on my bare skin sent a wave of heat through me, and the fact that his head was between my legs had me feeling a little distracted. I tried to stay focused, but more than once I caught myself running my fingers through his messy hair as he moved around effortlessly, despite the fact that he was carrying me on his shoulders.

We strung the lights up around the deck and patio and hung paper lanterns from the pergola where we would arrange the tables and chairs. The outdoor bar was already set up, and of course, my parents had left the grill pristine after the last time they'd used it. Jake and I chatted while we worked, and I was surprised at how easy it was for us to talk to each other. We kept the conversation casual, steering clear of any sensitive subjects, but it was still good to know that we could remain friendly.

When we finished setting up the patio, we hopped into Jake's truck and went to the store to pick up the beer and other alcohol for the party. As we drove along the tree-lined streets we were both quiet, and the air was thick with the tension of all that remained unsaid between us. We had been alone together in this truck a million times before, but it was all so different now.

"So, how does it feel being home?" Jake asked, breaking the silence.

"It's taking some getting used to. I don't think I realized how much I missed it here while I was away. It's been a long time." Glancing over at him from the passenger side, I couldn't help but notice the empty space between us. I always used to ride in the middle seat so I could be right next to him, and Jake would keep one hand on my leg, removing it only when he had to shift gears, and then putting it right back. I yearned to feel that comfort, and I had to fight the urge to move over and fill the space.

I was drifting into dangerous territory, so I shifted my gaze forward and tried to move on to more comfortable topics. "Are you excited for the wedding?"

"Yeah, I still can't believe they're getting married. It feels like just yesterday we were all stupid kids sneaking out in the middle of the night to meet up and do Lord knows what," he chuckled.

"If my parents had ever known what I was doing, they would've shipped me off!" I laughed. "The one time they did catch me, I pretended to be sleepwalking. I still don't know how I got away with that one."

"As I recall, you were the sneakiest one of us all, Miss Montgomery. Underneath that angel face was a stubborn little trouble-maker, just dying to get out. It was one of my favorite things about you."

My throat tightened when I thought about the girl that I used to be. The girl I'd left behind. Back then I was carefree, stubborn and spontaneous. I wasn't afraid to take chances or trust my gut.

Instead of over thinking things, I followed my heart and let my head take a backseat. What had happened to that girl? Now I was nothing but a pushover who went along with Daddy's plans and always played it safe. I felt like I'd become a disappointment to the girl I was before.

"Everything's different now," I said simply, looking out the window so he wouldn't see the sadness I was trying to hide.

"Not everything," he said.

Jake

We arrived back at Nora's house after picking up more than enough beer, wine and liquor to satisfy our get-together. After I parked my truck out front, Nora hopped into the back and started handing me the heavy boxes so I could bring everything into the house. When it was all unloaded, she stood on the tailgate, holding her hand out to me for balance as she hopped to the ground. Instead of grabbing her hand, I glanced up and wrapped my arms around her thighs to lift her, letting her body slide down mine until her feet touched the ground. I kept my hands on her hips, locking my eyes on hers so she would know exactly what was coming.

"Jake–don't," she stammered but didn't pull away.

"I have to," I told her, leaning forward and gently placing my lips on hers. I held them there for just a moment before pulling back to look at her. My heart felt like it was beating out of my chest.

"I–I can't do this, Jake."

"Then don't kiss me back."

I bent in to kiss her again, tightening my arms around her. Cautiously I moved my lips against hers and brought my hand up to touch her face, running my thumb over her cheek. She moaned softly against my lips, and it was all the encouragement I needed. When I felt her lips part for me, I let my tongue find hers and tilted her head, deepening the kiss. As my lips began moving more intensely, she wound her arms around my neck and crushed her body against mine.

The need I felt for her turned me completely inside out. I hadn't planned on kissing her today, but when I looked up at her standing on the tailgate, illuminated from the light of the setting sun, I knew I couldn't wait. I needed to figure out what it was that I was feeling. If it was something real, or just remnants of the past clouding the present. Still, I wasn't expecting this. Instead of curbing my appetite for her, it only intensified it. I'd never needed anything as much as I needed Nora.

When I finally pulled away, I brushed my thumb along her jaw and tucked a loose strand of hair behind her ear. "God, I missed you, Nora."

"This doesn't change anything," she said breathlessly. "I still have to go back to New York."

"We'll see," I said.

I devoted the next few days to working on the fishing cabin. It was actually starting to look halfway decent. I'd finished the exterior walls, put new shingles on the roof, and now I was focusing on the inside. It had always been more of a shelter than a place that anyone could actually stay in, but I was planning to change that. I'd put up sheetrock, painted the walls and started laying down new flooring. The plumbing and electric were old, but thankfully, they were still functional. I would squeeze a mini-fridge under the small bit of counter space next to the sink, and there were two burners that could be used for cooking. The small wood stove that had been here since my family bought the place was ancient, but it was functional and only needed a good cleaning.

On the opposite wall, I built an oversized window seat that was just big enough for two people to sleep. It had white wood panels and two drawers underneath to store blankets and pillows. I hoped that by the time I was finished, this would be the kind of place that our family and friends could actually spend a few days in.

I was putting a second coat of paint on one of the walls inside when I heard my dad pull up in his old work truck. Setting my paintbrush down, I went outside to meet him.

"I thought I might find you here," he said, climbing up the stairs to the small porch. "It's really coming along, I can barely recognize the place."

"It's getting there," I replied, taking a seat in one of the deck chairs. "A few more full days of work, and it might actually be ready." My dad sat down in the chair next to me, and I could tell he had something on his mind. "So what's goin' on, Pops?"

"I ran into Nora at the grocery store today," he said, eyeing me curiously. "You never told me she was back in town."

"Yeah, she came back for the wedding, but it doesn't sound like she plans to stick around. Did you talk to her?"

"Of course I did. You know how much I adore that girl. She's the only one who ever managed to set you straight. Seems to have done pretty well for herself in New York. Just as beautiful as ever too…"

"Yup." I knew what exactly what he was getting at.

"So, anything going on with you two?"

"I don't really know," I answered honestly.

"Well, are you going to find out?" he persisted. "I mean, do you still have feelings for her?"

I paused, taking a deep breath before answering. "Maybe… I don't know… is it crazy if I do? It's been four years. At this point she's been out of my life longer than she was in it. It doesn't make any sense."

"Jake," he chuckled. "Didn't anyone ever tell you that love doesn't make any sense? Sometimes when you meet the right person, you just know, and you stop looking for anything else 'cause you know you already found her."

"You make it sound so simple," I mumbled, focusing my gaze on the ground. "But Nora and me, it's way too complicated."

"Maybe it doesn't have to be. If you do love her, don't let her go this time."

Somehow my dad always managed to surprise me. I'd been a wreck after Nora left, but I always thought he was oblivious to most of the stuff that was going on with me. Then, boom – he comes at me with words of wisdom like this. I'd never told him what really happened with Nora and me, but somehow, I think he knew.

"Oh, and Jake…" he continued. "You are, and always were, good enough for her. Don't let anyone make you think otherwise."

"No, I wasn't good enough for her," I said, shaking my head. "At least, not before. I was a stupid kid. I should've gotten my act together sooner. I knew what I had, and I knew she deserved better than me."

"You may have been a little rough around the edges back then, but you loved that girl more than anything. That much was obvious. And now look at you. You're a hard worker and you've done real well for yourself. I'm proud of you, Jake."

I had no idea how my dad knew so much about all the things I thought I'd kept hidden, but I sure was glad he did.

chapter four

Nora

When the day of the party arrived, most of my morning was spent on finishing up last minute details and errands. Once everything was prepared for the party, I went upstairs to take a shower and start getting *myself* ready.

I wore my down hair in gentle waves, clipped up on one side, and opted for a little more makeup than usual. The pale yellow cocktail dress I'd chosen fell just above my knees, complimenting my tan skin, and I wore it with strappy heels and simple drop earrings.

Not too bad, I thought to myself when I looked in the mirror.

By the time the guests began to show up, I was in full-on hostess mode, greeting people, getting drinks and putting food onto plates. I was so preoccupied that I almost didn't notice Jake arrive. I'd been avoiding him since the kiss. I wasn't quite sure how to act around him. As much as I wanted to pretend like it didn't happen, I knew that would be impossible.

"Hey, gorgeous," he said, moving toward me with a huge grin spread across his face. "Do you ever look less than amazing?"

I smiled, trying to stay casual and ignore the butterflies fluttering around in my stomach. "You're not looking so bad yourself. In fact, you clean up pretty nice."

He was wearing khaki pants and a blue button-up shirt that matched his eyes. His normally messy hair was brushed back neatly, but he still had the light stubble along his jaw line that I'd always loved. He was so handsome that I got flushed just looking at him.

Jake didn't waste any time before jumping in to help me put all the food out, and even offered to man the grill while I tended to the guests. Things were in full swing when Susie arrived with Ethan. She looked spectacular in a short white dress with her shiny blonde hair in a loose, low bun. She looked so happy she was practically glowing, and I knew that she was going to be a beautiful bride.

Surprise flooded her expression when she walked out onto the patio and saw what Jake and I had set up, and I couldn't help but feel proud of what we had managed to put together for them. The twinkle lights and paper lanterns made it look truly magical.

"Nora!" Susie exclaimed, rushing over to hug me. "This is amazing. You have completely outdone yourself. I love it!"

"It really does look incredible," Ethan echoed, wrapping an arm around my shoulder and giving it a slight squeeze.

"I can't take all the credit," I said. "Jake was my co-party planner, after all."

"Well, well, well," Susie said with a knowing grin. "Glad to see you kids are getting along."

"Yeah, Sus, we're friends," I replied matter-of-factly, making sure to emphasize the word *friends*. I wasn't sure if I were reminding her or myself. The line I'd drawn between Jake and me was getting a little blurry, but nothing had really changed.

"If you say so!" she called over her shoulder as she went off to mingle.

Jake stayed busy on the grill, but every once in a while, he'd catch my eye from across the room and flash me a smile or wink playfully at me. I did my best to ignore him as I walked around and spoke to the guests, introducing myself to people I'd never met before and catching up with the ones I hadn't seen since before I'd left for school. When I finally grew tired of answering the same questions and felt I'd done my duty, I got myself a drink and sat down in a quiet corner of the patio to relax for a moment. It wasn't long before I saw Carter approaching, wearing an impeccable black suit that led me to believe he had come straight from the office. My dad certainly kept his associates busy over there. It was a bit discouraging to think that in a few short years, I would be one of them. My future would consist of long hours at the office, limited free time, and a life revolving around work.

"Hey Nora," Carter said with a smile, lowering himself into the chair next to mine. "This is quite the bash you put together. Thanks again for inviting me."

"I'm glad you made it. How are things?" He seemed much less tense when he was outside the office, and it helped put me at ease. I might be the boss's daughter, but while I was working at the firm, Carter would be the one I reported to. I wanted to make a good impression.

"Not too bad," he replied. "We're all looking forward to having you in the office. I can't tell you how badly we need the extra help. With your father away, the work is really starting to pile up!"

"I bet it is! And I'm guessing my dad is calling in non-stop, trying to micromanage every little thing even though he's supposed to be on vacation. It drives my mother crazy!"

"That explains a few things," he chuckled. "He talks so quietly on the phone, like he's sneaking around, and every once in a while he abruptly hangs up, like he just got caught."

I couldn't help but laugh, reminded of all the family vacations we'd had growing up where my father had done the same thing. He had been a workaholic for as long as I could remember, and my mom practically had to force him to relax.

Carter was surprisingly easy to talk to, and I found myself actually enjoying the conversation. He gave me some tips and advice about law school and even told me some funny childhood stories about Ethan and his brother that had me bent over laughing. He seemed like a good guy, and I was relieved to know that I would actually have a friend at the office while I was there.

I didn't realize how long we'd been sitting there talking until I looked up and saw that the party crowd had begun to thin out. After promising him that I would stop by the office in the next few days, I excused myself so I could devote my attention to the other guests. When I looked over at the grill to find Jake, I saw that he had nicely cleaned up and put the food away, but was nowhere to be found.

"Have you guys seen Jake?" I asked Susie and Ethan. I saw them glance at each other and immediately knew something was up. "What, did he leave?"

"Nah, I don't think he left," Ethan said. "But he disappeared shortly after you started cozying up to your new friend Carter."

"Carter works at my dad's firm, I was just being friendly!" I said defensively. "Besides, it's not like Jake and me are together. He gave up the right to get possessive a long time ago."

"Oh come on, Nora ... you know how he feels about you."

"Do I?" I was starting to get annoyed with them. "How am I the bad guy here? He's the one who deserted me and broke my damn heart."

"He didn't have a choice," Ethan mumbled, staring down at his feet.

"What do you mean, he didn't have a choice?" Now I was really confused. Why were they so adamant in defending him? I mean, I could understand why Ethan would defend Jake – they were best friends – but Susie wasn't saying a word to back me up.

She peered up at Ethan with a pleading look in her eyes, as if asking permission to say something, but they both remained silent.

"Listen," I snapped. "I understand that you two are hell-bent on getting Jake and me back together so we can relive our glory days of high school and live happily ever after, but it's not happening!" I knew I was being harsh, but I was totally fed up with this whole situation and their vague comments that made no sense whatsoever. "In case you forgot, Jake is the one who ended it. Not me. Just because he suddenly has lingering feelings for me doesn't mean I'm going to forget that he didn't love me enough to stay with me when I went off to school, or the decency to even say goodbye–"

"HE WENT TO NEW YORK!" Susie blurted out, practically yelling. She looked apologetically at Ethan, clearly recognizing that she'd said something she wasn't supposed to.

I stood there completely dumbfounded. "He went to New York?" I said, finally finding my voice. "Why... when?"

"Just a short while after you left," Ethan told me. "You have to talk to him though, Nora."

Susie gave me a quick hug, and then they left, leaving me alone to process this new information. Obviously, I had to find Jake and figure out what was going on.

When I went out to the driveway, I saw that his truck was still there, so I knew he was around somewhere. I checked in all the rooms of the house, and when I still didn't find him, I went back outside to the patio. Many of the guests were already gone, and there was still no sign of Jake. Looking out to the long dock that went over the marsh and out to the river, I squinted, searching for him in the darkness. I couldn't see anything, but I knew he was there.

As I walked away from the lights of the patio, my eyes began to adjust to the dark, and I could make out a figure standing at the end of the dock. As I got closer, I could tell that it was Jake. He was hunched over the rail looking out toward the water. When I approached him, he tilted his head toward me but didn't turn around. Once I was a few feet behind him, I stopped.

"Why didn't you tell me?" I asked.

He turned around to face me, ignoring my question.

"Why did you go to New York, Jake?"

"Isn't it obvious?" he said, finally looking me in the eyes.

"Not to me."

"I went there because I loved you." He took a step toward me. "Damnit, Nora... I still do. I don't care that it's been four years, I still feel exactly the same as I–"

Before he could finish, I crushed my lips against his and looped my arms around his neck. Within seconds, his arms were around my waist, pulling me toward him, and he was kissing me with the same passion and fury that I had.

In that moment, I could feel all the walls that I'd built up around me over the last four years begin to crack and crumble. Everything about it just felt... right. For the first time since I left Beaufort, I felt like I was exactly where I was supposed to be.

Our heated exchange eventually turned into a gentle embrace as our kisses slowed and our grasp on each other loosened. He ran a hand down my arm, leaving a trail of heat from his touch and held the side of my face as he tenderly kissed me. My legs felt like jello, and with each caress of his lips and touch of his hand, the warmth inside me grew until I felt like I could burst into flames. It had been so long since I felt like this, and I didn't want it to end. Pulling back just enough so I could look him in the eyes, I leaned my forehead against his.

"I missed you, too," I whispered.

Jake

Nora and I walked hand-in-hand back down the dock to rejoin the few remaining guests on the patio. I'd been so wrapped up in Nora that I'd almost completely forgotten about the party going on a few hundred feet away. I knew that we still had a lot to talk about, and she would need an explanation, but it would have to wait until we were alone.

While she went off to say her goodbyes to the people who were still lingering around, I cleaned up the last remnants of the party. I caught sight of Ethan and Susie on their way out and waved goodbye to them from across the patio. Judging from the ridiculous grins on their faces when they waved back to me, I knew they'd seen Nora and me holding hands. I assumed that they had clued her in about my trip to New York, and even though that wasn't how I'd wanted her to find out, at that moment I was way too damn happy to care.

Once everything was cleaned up, I sat down in one of the lounge chairs by the pool to wait for Nora. I couldn't help the smile on my face as I watched her, and when she looked over and caught my eye, she smiled coyly at me in a way that made me want to run over and take her in my arms again. God, she was beautiful.

After the last few people left, Nora came over to sit next to me. I took her hand in mine, caressing my thumb over hers.

"Finally," I said, smiling at her.

She smiled back at me, but I knew she had questions for me, so I stayed silent and let her ask.

"I just don't understand," she said. "If you wanted to be with me, why didn't you show up that night like we planned? Did you just not want me... like that?"

I turned to her, gently pulling her chin toward me so that she would meet my gaze. "Nora, of course I wanted you like that. I wanted you more than I'd ever wanted anything. I only put it off so long because I loved you, and things were different with you. I'd never been with anyone who I actually loved and cared about before, and I didn't want to screw it up. Honestly, I'm amazed I was able to wait so long. I took a hell of a lot of cold showers during the time we were together."

"Then why?" she asked. "What happened?"

"Your dad," I sighed. I hadn't ever wanted to be the one to tell her this, but she deserved to know the truth.

"What about my dad?"

So, I told her everything.

That morning, four years ago, I'd woken up as soon as the sunlight began streaming in my windows. Normally I would have rolled over and gone back to sleep, but I was so excited that I jumped right out of bed.

I went to the fishing cabin to clean up and brought over some blankets and candles. If I had been able to afford it, I would have taken Nora to an expensive hotel or somewhere nice, but since this was all I had, I wanted to make it as special as possible, even though I knew she deserved better.

I could remember wondering to myself how a stupid sonofabitch like me had ever been lucky enough to get a girl like her. It had taken every ounce of willpower I possessed to keep myself from going too far with her, and the fact that she wanted it too made it about a zillion times harder. Still, I knew I had to take it slow.

Nora was special, and to be honest, I'd been nervous about going all the way with her. Sure, I'd been with a lot of girls before, but I'd never really cared about them, and I sure as hell hadn't been in love with them. It wasn't going to be my first time, but it was going to be the first time it actually meant something. With Nora, it wasn't just sex. It was a hell of a lot more. I loved her.

A few hours before I was supposed to pick her up, I stopped

by her house to drop something off. I knew she'd probably be in the shower or busy getting ready, so I left it on her front porch where I knew she would see it. It was in a small box wrapped with silver wrapping paper, and I'd had the woman at the store use blue ribbon because it was Nora's favorite color. It was something I'd had my eye on it for months, and I'd finally saved up enough to buy it. I couldn't wait for Nora to open it.

As I was walking back to my car, Nora's father popped out of nowhere.

"Jake, what are you doing here?"

"Hi, Mr. Montgomery. I was just dropping something off for Nora. I'm not picking her up until later on, but I wanted to make sure she got it beforehand."

He frowned. "Seems a little silly to be buying gifts for a girl who's about to head off to New York and out of your life, don't you think?"

"Well, she certainly won't be out of my life," I said, trying to hide my aggravation. "We're going to make it work."

"Do you really think that's fair to Nora?" he questioned. "She's dreamed her whole life of going to school in New York, and now she's going to throw it all away for some boy who's content to stay here and do nothing but pound nails for the rest of his life?"

His words caught me completely off guard. The man had barely said two words to me since I'd met him. I knew that he didn't like me much, but I never expected this. I should have been furious, but I was too stunned to even respond... so I just stood there.

"Listen up," he continued. "Nora has a chance at a real future. She's worked hard for it, and I'm not going to let you stand in her way. She deserves better than you, and I think you know that. Deep down she knows it too, but she's too scared to say it because she thinks she loves you. If you care about her at all, you'll stay away from her."

"I'm not going anywhere," I said through gritted teeth, curly my fists at my sides, trying to contain the rage that was building inside me.

"No, you're not," he said. "But Nora is, and you will let her go. I know the kind of trouble you've gotten yourself into, and I know every cop and judge in this town. It wouldn't take much to unleash a whole lot of problems for you. So, the way I see it, you can choose to stay away from my daughter on your own, or I can make you stay away. Either way it's over. Am I making myself clear?"

Without a word I'd hopped into my truck and peeled out of the driveway. Anger was pumping through my veins, and I could barely even see where I was going. Somehow I made it to the cabin, where I quickly cleared out all the stuff I'd brought over earlier and threw it into the back of my truck. I drove until I ran out of gas, and then walked until I found a fleabag motel to stay in. My only stop was to buy a bottle of whiskey along the way. I had no idea where I was, or even how long I was there. All I'd wanted to do was numb the pain, but when I reached the bottom of the bottle, I still hadn't found any relief from my agony.

When I finally emerged from my drunken fog, I got back to my truck and started the drive back home. I hated Nora's father for pushing me around like he had and treating me like dirt. If anyone else had said that shit to me, they would have ended up in intensive care. Of course, that was part of the problem. If I hadn't been such a jackass for so many years, he wouldn't have been able to threaten me like that. That part was my own fault. I'd done some stupid shit, but he had to know that I would never stand in Nora's way. I loved her.

By the time I reached Beaufort, I was determined to go back and prove that to him. I wouldn't let him, or anyone, decide our fate. After stopping home for a quick shower and change of clothes to get rid of the whiskey stench, I went back to Nora's.

She was already gone.

When I was finished I looked over at Nora, and her eyes were full of tears. She pulled her hand from mine, burying her face in both hands as she cried. It broke my heart all over again to see her like this, and it was exactly why I didn't want to tell her. Her dad meant so much to her, and she'd worked so hard all her life to make him happy.

"How could he do that to me?" she cried. "He knew how much I loved you!"

I wrapped my arms around her and held her while she sobbed. After a while her cries began to fade and she leaned back to look at me, unshed tears still in her eyes.

"My whole life I did everything he wanted, went along with all his plans for me. The only decision I ever made for myself was being with you, and he took that away too."

"We're here now," I said, running my thumb along her cheek to wipe her tears away. "It doesn't matter how we got here, right?"

"But all that time…"

"Maybe it was for the best." She gave me a confused look so I tried to explain. "A couple weeks after you left, I went to New York. I was going to explain what happened and get you back, despite everything your father said. I made it all the way up to your campus, but when I got there I realized that your father was right. At least, about some things."

"That's not true! I never cared about any of that superficial crap. All I ever wanted was you!"

"I know that, but you deserved better. New York is… amazing. As I was walking around, it didn't take long for me to realize that it had a lot more to offer you than I did. I wanted you to be able to experience it and take advantage of every opportunity it would give you. So, I turned around and went home. I enrolled in classes over at UNC Beaufort, and I was determined to make something of myself and be the type of guy that you deserved. I wanted to be able to offer you everything. I figured that when you came home for the summer, I would have a chance to win you back ... but you never came back."

"Until now," she said, looking like she was going to burst into tears all over again.

"Nora, I didn't deserve you back then. Hell, I still don't deserve you now! But at least now I can offer you something. It broke my heart to leave New York without you, and losing you was the hardest thing I've ever gone through. But I know it was the right decision. Maybe now we have a real chance."

Under the twinkling lights of the patio I held her in my arms, not moving until I heard her yawn. When I was with Nora, it felt like time stood still, and I hadn't realized how late it was. I walked her inside and promised to see her tomorrow.

I couldn't believe the night had turned out the way it had. When I had seen her sitting with Carter, talking and laughing, I'd felt like my heart was splintering in my chest. I thought that was it. Instead, I actually had another chance, and I wasn't going to blow it. We had our (sort of) first date tomorrow, and I wanted it to be incredible. If I got her back, I wouldn't lose her again.

chapter five

Nora

I was still reeling over what my parents had done. They'd always been pushy, but I continually reasoned that it was only because they had high hopes and wanted the best for me. Stupidly, I'd assumed they wanted me to be happy. Never in a million years had I considered that they would do something so manipulative and destructive to deliberately cause me pain. They had seen firsthand how heartbroken I was over Jake, and they never said a word. Never once had they given me any indication that they were to blame for my unhappiness. Even after years had passed, they stayed silent. I wasn't sure how I could ever forgive them for this. I'd never been so furious or felt so betrayed.

My first instinct was to get them on the phone and demand an explanation, but I held back. They would be home in the next week or so, and this was something I needed to do face-to-face. After a lifetime of giving in to their demands and meeting their high expectations, it was time that I finally stood up for myself.

My eyes drifted to the guitar that sat in the corner of my bedroom. I walked over and kneeled in front of it, running my hands over the black case and popping it open for the first time in what seemed like forever. I took it out and sat down at my desk chair, surprised at how natural it still felt to hold it after all this time. I gently strummed the strings, tuning and reacquainting myself with it. For a while, I sat there in the warm glow of the morning sun, just playing around with different tunes, my eyes closed, enjoying the sound.

When Jake pulled into the driveway that evening to pick me up for our "first date," I had no idea what to expect. I put on a cute white sundress and carried my denim jacket with me in case it got cooler as the night went on. When Jake stepped up to the front door, I was relieved to notice that he was also dressed semi-casually, wearing a nice pair of jeans and a white button-up shirt. A wide smile spread across his cheeks when he saw me, and his eyes devoured me in a way that sent a tingle crawling up my spine.

Without giving any details of the evening away, he walked me to his truck and opened the passenger side door, helping me as I climbed in. I had a nervous, excited feeling in the pit of my stomach, and I could sense that he felt the same way. We weren't kids anymore, and it made this whole thing seem a lot more real.

I had to wonder if after all these years, we might not be as compatible as we'd been before. What if we'd outgrown each other? At one point in time, we'd known each other better than anyone else, but four years had passed, and in a lot of ways we were different people now. Were we kidding ourselves with the idea that we could have anything even remotely close to what we'd had before?

Silence stretched across the cab as we pulled out of the driveway. Every few minutes we would sneak glances at each other, until eventually Jake's face broke into a grin.

"What's with all this weirdness between us?" he laughed. "It's not like we haven't done this before."

I let out a breath, laughing as I shook my head. "I have no idea! I guess we have to work on getting comfortable with each other again."

"Well then we'll probably have to spend a lot of time together." His eyes twinkled mischievously as he peeked over at me. "Think you might be up for that?"

"Sounds tough," I said, grinning back at him. "But I think I'll manage."

Jake drove to Waterfront Park and found an open space in the parking lot. He walked alongside me as we moved down the long brick and stone walkway that ran along the water. Eventually, we arrived at a restaurant that I'd never seen before. It looked nice, and judging by the number of patrons, it seemed to be a popular spot.

"This place opened up a year or so ago, but it's become a local favorite," Jake said as he led me inside. "I figured it was about time I took you to a nice dinner, considering that in high school my idea of that was grabbing a pizza and eating in the back of my pickup."

"Hey!" I said, elbowing him playfully. "I happened to enjoy those dinners."

"Me, too," he winked. "But let's see if I can do a little better this time around."

I was surprised when he informed the hostess that he had a reservation, and I smiled to myself at the fact that he had actually put some thought into our date.

We were seated at a small table near the window with a gorgeous view of the setting sun over the river. By the time we had our drinks, we had settled into easy conversation. Any earlier tension between us had faded, replaced with the same comfort we used to have. Jake always had a way of making me feel at ease, whether we were in serious conversation or just joking around. I told him about my life in New York, and he updated me on what had been going on in Beaufort and about getting his degree in architecture. I loved hearing him talk about architecture. The way he spoke was so passionate, and it was obvious that he really knew his stuff.

In a way, it was hard for me to believe that this was the same Jake who used to steal golf carts from the course to go joyriding and threw parties in the field behind the high school principal's house when he was away on vacation. Even though I'd always known that he had the potential to do something really great, as I sat there listening to his visions and ideas, I couldn't help but feel proud of him.

"How's the songwriting?" he asked. "Are you still playing?"

"I took a bit of a hiatus," I admitted with a shrug. "I played for a little while today, though, and it all came right back."

He looked at me with a questioning gaze but didn't say anything. I guess I could understand his confusion. Before I'd left, music was everything to me. I had needed to play and write almost as much as I needed to breathe. It was where I found my peace and sanity.

"You sounded so good at the bar the other night," he said. "I just assumed you were still at it."

"It's easy to sound good when I'm singing someone else's songs. When it comes to singing my own, it's a different story."

"You always used to play your songs for me."

"You didn't count!" I laughed.

"Ouch!" He feigned a hurt expression.

"You know what I mean. That was different. Besides, most of my songs were about you, so it was only fair that you got to hear them."

"Well, people out there don't know what they're missing. You're incredible."

I blushed, trying to remember if I'd always been this self-conscious around him. Probably. Jake affected me like no one else. Still, as much as I appreciated what he said, I knew that performing my own songs just wasn't in the cards for me. The songs I wrote were too personal. I would be far too nervous singing them in front of an audience. All I'd ever wanted was to turn on the radio and hear an amazing artist singing the songs I'd written. But that was a silly childhood dream.

After we finished our dinner and Jake paid the check, we walked out of the restaurant. Darkness had settled over the city and the sky had become a vibrant blue; illuminated by the flashes of light from the street lamps lining the walkway. Jake reached for my hand, weaving his fingers with mine as he led me further along toward the park. It was the first time he'd touched me all evening, and the feel of his hand in mine sent a chill through my body that had nothing to do with the cool night air.

"So is there anything else on the agenda for tonight?" I asked, unable to contain my curiosity about what else he might have in store for us.

"Absolutely," he smiled at me. "I figured that since you've been away from Beaufort for so long, I would take it upon myself to re-introduce you to the place. Our next stop is just a little ways up ahead."

Even though I'd been back in town for over a week, I'd been so busy with the party that I hadn't had a chance to do much, so I couldn't wait to see what was in store for us next. The fact that Jake had planned all of this made it even more exciting.

I heard a song in the distance, and Jake steered us toward the grassy amphitheater where live music was coming from a small stage. It wasn't crowded; mostly occupied by people who had stopped to listen for a few minutes before continuing along to the bars and restaurants. In the center there were families who had their blankets laid out for a picnic, while the kids ran around playing and chasing each other. It was the perfect place to be on a night like this.

We sat down on the stairs near the side, facing the stage. I closed my eyes and listened to the sound of the instruments and the flawless voice that was singing along with them. I leaned into Jake and rested my head on his shoulder, breathing him in and relishing in the feel of him next to me.

"This is… perfect," I sighed. "I can't even remember the last time I did this."

"I'm glad you like it." He squeezed my hand gently, rubbing his thumb against mine in a way that gave me goose bumps.

For a long time we sat there in silence, just enjoying the music and being with each other. When the band announced that they were taking a break, we finally broke out of the trance and got up from our seats. After buying ice cream from the stand nearby, we sat down on one of the bench swings that lined the walkway facing the water. Jake rested his arm on the back of the seat behind me, caressing my bare shoulder with one hand while he held his ice cream cone in the other.

When we finished our ice cream I felt him move a little closer to me. I turned to face him, pointing to the corner of his mouth. "You've got a little ice cream, right… there."

"Oh, do I?" he responded, without making a move to wipe it away.

I could see the mischievous flicker in his eyes, and I knew that he was testing me. So far he'd been the one to make all the advances toward me, and now he was going to see if I would make a move. I loved this playful side of him. I was glad that he hadn't lost it and that he still wasn't afraid to test me or push my buttons.

"I guess I'll get it." I reached up, but instead of wiping away the ice cream, I brushed my fingers along his cheek and held them there. Resting my other hand on his leg, I slowly moved in to kiss him, encouraged by the excitement I saw in his eyes. As soon as my lips touched his, he moved his arm from the back of the seat and wrapped it around me, pulling me closer. I briefly took my lips off his and used my tongue to lick away the ice cream, causing him to growl hungrily as he took my mouth again in a deep kiss.

The feel of Jake's lips and hands on me made it easy to forget that, despite the cloak of darkness surrounding us, we were still in a public place. We pulled apart a little, catching our breath and making our embrace a little more PG-rated. He kept his arm around me, holding me close as we sat together on the swing, watching the headlights of cars crossing the bridge in the distance. I liked that we were able to sit together in comfortable silence and enjoy each other without feeling the need to fill in the gaps with mindless chit-chat.

The crisp May air grew colder, reminding us that it was getting late. Jake drove me home and left the engine running while he got out and walked me to the door.

"Planning for a quick getaway?" I teased.

"No, just keeping myself in check," he grinned. "You have a tendency to drive me a little wild, and if I park the car, I might never leave."

Knowing that I could make him feel that way gave me a sense of power, even though part of me wanted to drag him inside and into my bed. Whether he knew it or not, he'd always had the ability to drive me crazy, too.

After a brief kiss that left me wanting more, we said goodnight.

"See you soon?" I said.

"You bet you will," he answered, kissing me sweetly on the temple before turning to go back to his truck.

Jake

The day after my date with Nora was a workday, so I was out the door bright and early to go to the job site. I knew I had a ridiculous grin on my face for most of the day, but I couldn't help it. I didn't care that the other guys on the job kept giving me crap about it. I'd missed feeling this way. For the first time in a long time, I actually had something to look forward to.

By noon I finally caved and called Nora.

"Hello?" she answered on the third ring.

"Miss me yet?"

"Who's this?"

"The guy who took you on the best date of your life last night." I was pretty sure that she was only pretending that she didn't know it was me, since I'd given her my number already.

"You're going to have to be more specific," she teased. "I've been on an awful lot of dates lately."

Now I knew she was just playing with me. I loved how feisty she was, even if it meant she was constantly keeping me on my toes.

"Aw, shoot..." I said. "I guess I'll have to step up my game. Think maybe you could give me another chance to impress you?"

"What did you have in mind?"

"Are you free tonight? Maybe 7ish?"

"I suppose I could pencil you in."

"Well thank you, ma'am," I drawled. "But I'll be there no matter what, so you better put it in bold print."

I heard her laugh on the other end of the phone, and the sound alone gave me butterflies. I already missed her.

"See you tonight, Jake," she said before hanging up.

I shoved my phone into the pocket of my jeans and started walking back toward the house we were working on. Halfway there I stopped, took my phone back out, and typed a quick text to Nora.

Can't wait :)

Satisfied, I got back to work. I'd never in my whole life been a mushy or romantic type of guy, but Nora managed to bring it out in me. I didn't even care how pathetic I was acting. If this was my last shot, I was damn well gonna give it my all.

We finished up work a little early, so I stopped at my parents' house on the way home. I could smell dinner cooking as I approached the front door, and when I walked in, I found my mom in the kitchen chopping vegetables.

"Hey, Ma," I said, walking into the kitchen.

"Jake! What a pleasant surprise!" She turned around to give me a hug and a kiss on the cheek. "Your dad is just outside turning the grill on for steaks. Are you staying for dinner?"

"Thanks, but I have plans tonight," I said, reaching to grab a beer from the fridge and trying to conceal the excitement on my face. I couldn't hide anything from my mom. She could read me like a book.

"Oh, that's nice. What are you doing?"

"Plans with Nora?" my dad said, sneaking around the corner, holding a spatula. He winked at me before coming up behind my mom, planting a kiss on her cheek and grabbing a piece of carrot she had just finished chopping.

John and Eileen Harris had been happily married for twenty-five years, and they had no problem showing it. So I was used to all their kissing and groping. It had grossed me out when I was younger, but now I was just glad that they were still so happy together after so many years. I wanted to have that.

"Nora Montgomery?" My mom spun around enthusiastically. "You're seeing Nora?"

"Thanks, Dad."

"Jake, honey, you must bring Nora by the house!" my mom exclaimed. "It's been far too long. I've missed that girl! Are you two back together? Oh, I hope so!"

I glared at my dad, who just stood there laughing at what he had knowingly unleashed on me by bringing up Nora. My parents adored her, especially my mom. When we were together, Nora was like the daughter she'd never had, so it was no surprise that my mom was ecstatic at the idea of us being together again.

"It's only our second date, so don't start picking out china patterns just yet," I said.

My mom gave me a knowing look. They knew me well enough to know that anything involving Nora was a big deal. Second date or not.

I stayed for a few more minutes to finish my beer and help my dad get the steaks on the grill before leaving to get ready. I was barely three steps out the door when I heard my mom yelling at me from inside.

"Don't mess it up this time!"

After showering and putting on a clean pair of jeans and a t-shirt, I still had a lot of time to kill before leaving to pick up Nora. I was anxious to see her again, but I didn't want to show up early in case she was still getting ready. After staring at the clock for a few minutes, I took Max outside and threw the ball for him a dozen times. When I went back inside, the clock had barely moved.

Okay, you gotta chill out, I told myself.

I sat down on the couch and began flipping through the television channels as I attempted to pass the time. *24 minutes to go.* I heard my cell phone chime with a new text message. Hoping it was Nora letting me know she was ready, I practically lunged for the phone on the coffee table. It wasn't Nora. The name that did appear on the screen was not one that I wanted to see.

Aw, shit.

Hey baby watcha doin 2night? Just got
back in town

I stared at the screen, trying to decide how to respond. Ethan's cousin, Lindsey, was a few years younger than us, and I'd made the horrendous mistake of hooking up with her a few times during one of my dark and depressive phases. Each time I'd been piss drunk, and the girl was nothing if not persistent, but I still should have known better. I'd tried letting her down nicely, and when that didn't work, I began to simply ignore her. Even then, she wouldn't quit. It hadn't been a problem when she was off at school, but now that she was back, I knew she was going to make things difficult for me.

Perfect timing.

Ethan knew about the whole situation, and though he obviously wasn't thrilled, he cut me some slack because he knew what Lindsey was like. Of course, it didn't stop him from giving me grief about it any chance he got. As understanding as Ethan was, the fact remained that Lindsay was his family, so I couldn't just tell her off, no matter how badly I wanted to. Before Nora came back into the picture, I just ignored Lindsey, but now that Nora was in my life again, everything was different. She was already somewhat of a flight risk, and now I was terrified that Lindsey would do something to mess things up.

I was sure Nora would understand if I explained everything to her. It wasn't like she expected that I was celibate the whole time she was away, just as I didn't expect that of her. But it was too soon, and things were still so new and delicate between us. I wasn't ready to throw a wrench in it just yet. I'd never had feelings for Lindsay—and I never would—but I'd been in a bad place at the time it happened.

The real problem was that Nora knew Lindsey from high school, and they had never gotten along. Actually, they'd hated each other. Lindsey had always had a thing for me, and when I started dating Nora, she'd gone out of her way to try and get between us. Not to mention that Lindsey was, well… crazy. If she caught wind that Nora and I were seeing each other again, I knew she would be a problem. As if there weren't already enough obstacles in our way. I would definitely have to tread lightly with this one.

I was afraid that if I ignored Lindsay she would keep texting me all night, so I typed a quick response.

Sry, have plans.

I hoped that would deflect her for the night. Looking up at the clock I saw that it was almost seven o'clock, so I pushed my worry aside and focused on Nora.

I didn't tell Nora where we were going, so I was glad to see that she was dressed casually in jeans and a sweater. Not that it mattered what she wore, because the girl could go out wearing high-waisted mom jeans and a tie-dye shirt, and she would still have any straight guy within a two-mile radius drooling all over her.

When I pulled off the highway into the huge clearing where the drive-in movie theater was, I couldn't help but watch her expression as she realized where I was taking her.

"No way!" she said, her face lighting up in a huge smile. "This place is still open?"

"Of course it is. It's only the finest cinema in the state!"

"Well done, sir," she laughed. "You promised me memorable, and you most certainly delivered."

"Ask and you shall receive," I winked.

I let out the breath that I didn't realize I'd been holding, relieved that she was excited to be here. We'd loved coming here in high school, but even then it had been pretty run-down, and part of me had been worried that Nora might have preferred a classier date. The fact that she was so excited to be here just reinforced what I already knew: that deep down, she was still the same fun, free-spirited girl who was down for anything.

After pulling up to the booth and buying our tickets, I found a spot with the best view of the huge screen and backed my truck into the space, so it was facing away from the screen.

"Just like old times!" Nora said, laughing. We'd always watched the movies from the back of my pickup, and I was glad she remembered that.

"Even better than old times." I hopped out of the truck and opened the big bag I had stashed in the back. I pulled out the cushions that I'd borrowed from my parent's patio furniture and lined them along the bed of the truck so we'd be able to watch the movie in comfort.

"My, my, my… who knew Jake Harris was so suave?"

"Only the best for you, m'lady." I tipped my imaginary hat at her and enjoyed the adorable giggle that I got in return.

"Lucky me!"

We went to the concession stand and bought pizza, fries and two beers – all the elements of a well-balanced meal – and carried it back to the truck just as the previews started playing on the movie screen. I jumped up into the bed of the truck and held out my hand to help her climb in.

Once we were situated on the cushions, I watched her take a huge bite of her slice of pizza, closing her eyes like she was enjoying five-star cuisine.

"Mmm… so… good!" she managed to say as she chewed.

I couldn't help but laugh as I watched her. Unlike most girls, who would order a salad or pick delicately at a slice of pizza, Nora just dove right in without holding back. Another thing to add to the list of things I loved about her.

"Well, you can take the girl out of Beaufort, but you can't take the Beaufort out of the girl," I teased her. She ignored my comment and threw a french fry at me, laughing when it hit me square in the face.

We finished eating just in time for the beginning of the movie, so I threw our trash out and grabbed two more beers before climbing back into the truck. As I settled into the cushions with my back resting against the cab of the truck, Nora cuddled in next to me. I rested my hand on her thigh, and she automatically wrapped her arm around mine, gently stroking my forearm with her delicate fingers. It felt so natural, and in that moment, it seemed like no time had passed since we were together.

By the time it got dark, the air between us was practically crackling with electricity. The plot of the movie we were watching was a total blur because I couldn't focus on anything other than Nora being next to me. I knew she felt it, too. I could feel the heavy beat of her pulse and heard her sharp intake of breath when I slowly moved my hand to caress her thigh.

"I think this is the longest we've ever actually *watched* a movie," I whispered into her ear.

She giggled. "That's because you always had me on my back before the opening credits."

I squeezed her thigh gently. "I don't remember you ever complaining."

"Well, of course not. Why do you think I liked going to the movies so much?" She looked up at me as she used her tongue to moisten her full lips and then trailed her fingertips along the sensitive skin of my inner arm.

"You asked for it," I said, grabbing her by the waist and pulling her into my lap so she was sitting sideways against my chest. Leaning down, I pulled her chin toward me as she reached up and grabbed me by the collar of my t-shirt to pull me closer. Our lips met in a fierce kiss, fueled by the energy in the air and the desire that we had both been keeping at bay.

I kneaded her hip with one hand while I ran the other slowly up her thigh, then along the bare skin of her arm and the curve of her neck. She wrapped her arm around my back, pulling me closer to her as I deepened the kiss. Her hand slipped under the hem of my shirt, leaving a trail of heat as it moved up the muscles of my back. A groan escaped from my throat, and I hauled her against me until she was close enough to feel exactly how much I wanted her.

Nora showed no signs of slowing down, but I knew that if I didn't cool things off now, I would never be able to. As much as I wanted to drag her home to my bed and wrap myself up in her, my other brain –the one that wasn't in my pants– knew that I had to take this slow.

Gradually, our kiss became gentler, and we pulled back, both of us still catching our breath after our heated exchange. I readjusted her so she was between my legs with her back resting against my chest, and wrapped my arms around her waist while she wove our fingers together in her lap. Unable to resist, I swept her hair to one side, exposing her neck so I could brush my lips against her soft skin and inhale her sweet smell, trailing soft kisses from her shoulder to her temple while she hummed in appreciation.

The buzzing in my pocket from my cell phone was the only thing that kept it from being a perfect night.

After the movie was over, I drove Nora home and did my best not to get carried away again. When she turned to the door I could see that she was debating whether or not to invite me in, and I was relieved when she didn't. Not that I didn't want to. I just didn't think I would be able to keep myself from hauling her upstairs and doing things that I'd been dreaming about doing since the day I met her.

As I backed out of the driveway after dropping her off, I caught a glimpse of her watching through the window, and it tugged at my heart. No matter how much time I spent with Nora, it was never enough.

God, I was such a sucker.

chapter six

Nora

When I got into bed and closed my eyes, all I could think about was the feel of Jake's hands moving up my thigh and his lips trailing kisses along my neck. I still felt the blazing heat from his touch, and I couldn't quell my aching need for more. He'd always had this effect on me, and I couldn't help but feel irritated that he could so easily put a stop to things. I knew I wouldn't have been able to stop it–unless maybe someone had come over and hosed me down with cold water. And even then I still might not have stopped.

The next day I had plans with Susie to work on last-minute wedding details. After going for a quick run, I took a shower and changed into a floral sundress that would be appropriate for brunch with Susie and her mom. When I walked into the restaurant there was no sign of Susie, but as I scanned the people and tables, I saw Susie's mother waving at me from a table in the corner.

"Nora, darling, you look wonderful!" she said, pulling me in for a tight hug.

"Thank you, Helen, it's so good to see you!" I'd always been close to Susie's mother, so I was expected to call her by her first name. Helen and my mother were close friends, which was why Susie and I had been inseparable since we were in diapers.

"Susie just called to tell me that she's running a few minutes late," Helen explained. "But I'm glad to have a chance to catch up with you. How are you? You must be so glad to be back after all this time!"

"I'm very glad to be back," I told her, and for the first time the words actually felt true. "I wouldn't have missed this wedding for the world."

"I know how happy your mother is to have you home. It's all she's been talking about for months. I'm sure she's anxious to get back and see you. Are they enjoying their trip?"

When she mentioned my parents, I felt a huge lump forming in my throat. I was still beyond angry with them and had been avoiding their calls ever since I found out what they'd done.

"It sounds like they're having a lovely time," I finally answered. Fortunately, Susie came rushing through the dining room before I was forced to elaborate any further.

"Sorry I'm late!" she said breathlessly, as she practically fell into her chair. "Ethan and I had to work through a slight disagreement." Turning to me, she lowered her voice so only I could hear. "Then we had a little making up to do, if you know what I mean!" She winked.

I laughed at Susie's bluntness. It was one of my favorite things about her. She smiled mischievously while her mother examined the menu, oblivious to her daughter's most recent over-share.

With the wedding fast approaching, we had a ton of details to work out. While I was in New York, I hadn't been able to help out as much as I'd wanted to, so I was excited to finally be able to fulfill my maid-of-honor duties.

When we finished eating, Susie's mom excused herself to go say hello to one of her friends who was at a nearby table, giving Susie and me a few minutes of uncensored girl talk.

"So what happened with Ethan?" I asked her. "You two hardly ever fight. Is everything okay?"

"Oh, we're fine," she said, waving her hand dismissively. "It was stupid stuff. With the wedding so close, we're both just a little stressed and getting on each other's nerves."

"No cold feet or anything, right?" I probed, searching her face for any sign of hesitation.

"Hell, no," she grinned. "Every couple needs a good fight every now and then. Otherwise they would never get to experience mind-blowing make up sex!"

I kept my eyes fixed on my water glass, but I could feel her gaze burning into me. I knew exactly what was coming next.

"Speaking of hot sex," she continued. "How was your date with Jake last night? Please tell me you two finally spent some time between the sheets."

As much as I wanted to be annoyed with her, I knew she meant well, and I certainly couldn't blame her for being curious. We hadn't had much of a chance to talk about what was going on with Jake and me.

"It was great," I said. "No 'between the sheets' action though. Sorry to disappoint you."

"Lame!"

"It was only our second date, Sus!"

"Or like, your thousandth, depending how you look at it," she pointed out. "Does he still set your panties on fire?"

My flushed cheeks gave me away. I knew Susie could see it, so I didn't bother answering her question. I gave her a sly smile, ignoring her quiet laughter, and focused my attention on Helen as she made her way back to the table.

The next stop for Susie and me was the dress shop for our fittings. Susie had chosen her wedding dress and the bridesmaid dresses from a boutique that was owned by Ethan's aunt, and I couldn't wait to finally see what she had picked out.

"You better not be sticking me in some hideous dress," I joked as we entered the boutique.

"Ptff, never!" she scoffed. "Ethan's aunt helped me pick them out, and they are gorgeous. You should consider yourself lucky that you get to try yours on ahead of time. Since Kate and Mindy aren't coming until a few days before, they're stuck with what they get."

Susie's other bridesmaids, Kate and Mindy, were her friends from college. Luckily, we'd all spent a lot of time together over the years and we'd all become close, so there was no awkwardness between us.

We walked into the shop and saw Ethan's aunt, Sherry, rolling out a rack of dresses, presumably ours, neatly hung inside their dress bags.

"Hello, girls!" she greeted us happily. She was dressed in a chic pink dress accessorized with chunky pearl jewelry, and I could tell right away that we were in good hands. "I've got your dresses right here. Who wants go first?"

Susie went into the dressing room first and, with Sherry's help, got into her wedding dress while I waited anxiously on the couch for her to come out. When she finally strolled out and stood up on the small platform, I was rendered completely speechless.

"What do you think?" she said nervously, examining herself in the large mirror. The dress she'd chosen was a stunning white satin A-line gown with a sweetheart neckline and a fitted bodice that flared out slightly at the waist and fell to the floor in gorgeous waves. It wasn't a huge ball gown, but was simple and elegant.

"Absolutely perfect," I said, my eyes welling up with tears. "You look stunning!"

While Sherry poked and pinned Susie, making the final adjustments for her fitting, I went into the dressing room to change into my bridesmaid dress. While I was in there, I overheard Susie talking to someone who had come into the store. The voice sounded familiar to me, but I couldn't place it.

I hung up the dress bag and slowly pulled the zipper down, excited to see what Susie had chosen for me. When I opened the bag and saw it, I was thrilled, and loved it immediately. I stepped into the dress and gently pulled up the side zipper before turning to the mirror.

It was a beautiful mint-colored chiffon, floor length, with an empire waist and slight ruching along the sweetheart neckline.

"Gorgeous!" Susie squealed happily when I walked over to rejoin them, standing awkwardly on the platform while Sherry checked the fitting of the dress.

The door leading to the back of the store opened, and immediately I recognized whose voice I'd heard from inside the dressing room. It was Ethan's cousin, Lindsey.

Duh, of course. Sherry was her mother, but somehow I hadn't made the connection. I greeted her nicely, plastering on my kindest and most genuine smile, but all I got in return was a lukewarm 'hi' and a sarcastic smirk.

Lindsey had harbored a huge crush on Jake throughout high school. Although he'd never reciprocated her feelings, it didn't stop her from trying. She was always flitting around him in her skimpy little outfits with her bottle blonde hair, doing anything she could to make him notice her. Naturally, she hated me when I started dating Jake and took it upon herself to make me her enemy. I would've thought she'd be over it by now, but apparently her feelings for me hadn't changed one bit. Not that I cared. I rarely had to interact with her, and I knew that Susie only tolerated her because she had to. Even Ethan could hardly stand her.

Doing my best to ignore Lindsey, I stood patiently while Sherry measured, poked and prodded at the dress I was wearing. It already fit me perfectly, but Sherry decided to hem a little bit off the bottom so I wouldn't trip and face-plant on my way down the aisle. I liked Sherry a lot, and I couldn't help but wonder how two people who shared the same DNA could end up being so different.

When Susie came back from changing out of her wedding dress, I gave her an appreciative smile. "I love this dress. I never should have doubted you!"

"I told you!" she said cheerfully. "Wait until Jake sees you in this. We're going to need a forklift to pick his jaw up off the floor."

The second the words came out of Susie's mouth, Lindsey's head jerked up from whatever she was doing. The glare she gave us was unmistakable. I guess that answered my question about whether or not she was still lusting over Jake. Not that I could blame her, because Jake was gorgeous and amazing, but I would have thought she'd given up the chase by now. Clearly that girl had some attachment issues.

I almost laughed out loud when I said those words to myself. *Ha! Like you're one to talk!* I guess I'd never moved on either, unless a handful of bad dates in four years could be considered moving on.

Jake Harris was a tough act to follow.

By the time Susie and I were finished with all the errands on our wedding task list, the sun was already down, and I was exhausted. I perused the kitchen to find something to eat, and finally ended up making myself a peanut butter and jelly sandwich. I finished it off with a tall glass of milk and went upstairs for the night.

While I played with my guitar, I tried not to think about the fact that I already missed Jake even though I'd seen him less than twenty-four hours ago. Or what that meant. My original plan of "getting him out of my system" didn't seem to be working, and spending time with him only made me want to spend *more* time with him. I decided not to think about the future for a change. I would enjoy our time together without holding back, and when the summer was over, we could take it from there.

There was no way for me to avoid going back to New York for law school. I was already enrolled, and it was too late to transfer to another school. I couldn't drop out, because then what would I do? Getting my law degree and joining my dad's firm was the only future I'd ever known, and without it I had no direction to go in. The fact that I was angry with my father didn't change that.

Going back to New York was inevitable. So I ignored the fact that the mere thought of leaving here without Jake tied my stomach into knots.

Jake

It was an unseasonably hot day in Beaufort, and of course it was also the day that I had vowed to finish up the work at the fishing cabin. The air was hot and humid, and it wasn't long before my shirt clung to me with sweat.

As I laid new boards on the dock, I gazed longingly at the cool water below and groaned. I wanted nothing more than to jump in and cool myself off, but I had to finish.

Just a few more boards, then you can take a break.

I was in the middle of pounding a nail into one of the new boards when I felt my phone vibrate in my pocket. Putting down the hammer, I pulled out my phone to see who it was, and I think my heart literally stopped beating for a couple of seconds.

Pool party? ;)

It was from Nora, and along with the message was a picture she'd taken of herself that showed her from the neck down in a sexy-as-hell bikini, lounging in a chair by the pool.

Without a second's hesitation, I was packing up my tools and heading for my truck. Some things were more important than work.

I parked in Nora's driveway and walked around the side of the house, navigating my way through the towering oaks to get to the backyard. Nora was lounging on the patio at the edge of the pool, lying perfectly still with her eyes closed. Her skin was shiny with what looked like baby oil, and the tiny bikini she was wearing showcased her amazing body and perfect curves.

Instead of announcing my arrival, I quietly stripped down to my boxer briefs–I'd been in too much of a hurry to go home and get my swim trunks–and ran to the pool, executing a perfect cannonball into the water right next to where she was sitting.

"Eeeeek, Jake!" she shrieked, jumping up from her lounge chair as the water sprayed all over her. "I'm gonna kill you!"

"Oh, ya?" I teased, treading water in the middle of the pool. "You're gonna have to come in here and get me then."

Tossing her sunglasses onto the chair, she dove gracefully into the pool, eventually popping up right next to me. "Boo!"

Her long hair was slicked back, and her face glistened with droplets of water. Those gorgeous green eyes of hers were sparkling as they reflected off the glassy ripples on the surface of the water, stealing my breath from me. All I could do was stare at her. When I moved in closer she laughed, dipping back under the water and swimming in the opposite direction.

"Okay, now you're in trouble," I warned, swimming toward her.

We played around in the pool until I was out of breath and had no choice but to surrender.

"Gotcha!" she said, swimming up to me and wrapping her arms around my neck.

"You win." Putting my arms around her waist, I drew her in for a kiss. What I intended as a quick peck turned into much more when she opened her mouth, brushing my lips with her tongue. My body took over, pulling her against me as I explored every inch of her sweet mouth. When she moaned softly, it was like adding fuel to the fire.

I moved us over to the edge of the pool and pressed her up against the wall. As she tightened her arms around my neck and wrapped her legs around my waist, I slipped my hands under her perfect ass and hauled her against me, letting her feel how hard I was for her. A growl escaped from my throat, and I dropped my mouth to her neck, gently nibbling and sucking along her collarbone before moving back to her lips.

Nora rocked her hips against me, her warm center perfectly aligned with my hard length, as she moaned into my mouth.

"Aw, shit," I groaned. I knew I was in trouble. Each time she rocked, I got closer to the point of no return, but all I could think about was how damn good she felt.

"Baby, you gotta tell me to stop," I said, breathing heavily.

"Why?" she asked without stopping.

"'Cause if I don't hit the brakes right now, I'm afraid I won't be able to."

She lifted her head to look at me and then brought her mouth up to my ear. "Don't stop," she whispered, nibbling my ear in the way that she knew drove me crazy.

That was it. I turned off my brain and gave in to the pleasure that we both wanted. My lips found her neck while I used one hand to untie the strings on her bikini top. I let it fall and cupped her full breasts with both hands, squeezing them gently as her fingers clawed into my shoulders. Lowering my head, I took one in my mouth and gently sucked her nipple while I continued to massage her other breast with my hand.

"Ahhh, Jake…" she moaned, fisting a handful of my hair as she continued to grind her hips into mine.

I was completely lost in her. I wanted to touch her everywhere at once, to savor every inch of her body. My mouth continued to spread kisses all over her chest and cleavage while my greedy hands alternated between kneading her breasts and gripping her ass to pull her firmly against my erection. I wanted to touch her everywhere at once, and I loved the way she felt in my hands.

Nora was sliding her hand down my back into the waistband of my shorts when the sound of her cell phone ringing snapped me back to reality.

"You better get that," I said, removing my mouth from her chest.

"It's just Susie," she muttered, continuing to move her hand down my back.

I gave her a quick kiss on the lips and reluctantly began to untangle myself from her. "You know Susie doesn't like to be left waiting."

Grabbing her by the hand, I pulled her with me to the steps of the pool to climb out. The adorably frustrated look on her face as she re-fastened her top made me want to drag her back in and finish what we started, but I had to be strong. My first time with Nora would be special, and doing it in the shallow end of her parent's pool wasn't exactly what I had in mind.

Nora picked up her phone to call Susie back. "Should I tell them to come over?" she asked.

"Yeah, definitely." I looked down at the rock hard erection that had formed a massive tent in my boxers. Nora giggled, and I glanced up to see her eying it as well. Glad that she wasn't too mad at me for stopping things, I laughed.

"Tell Ethan to bring me some swim trunks. And could you please point me in the direction of a cold shower?"

As much as I liked spending time with Nora alone, I was glad that Susie and Ethan had come over to join us. It had been four years since we'd all hung out like this, but it was as though nothing had changed.

Ethan and I lounged poolside while the girls went inside to grab some food. "Man, I could get used to this," I said, basking in the rays of the hot sun.

"I know," Ethan agreed. "When do Nora's parents get back again?"

"Later this week, I think. Remember when they caught us here after homecoming? They came home early from some trip, and we weren't supposed to be here. I thought they were going to shoot me on sight."

"Uh, from what I remember, I'm pretty sure that they were pissed because we were drinking all their booze, and you were fondling their daughter in the pool... and you wonder why they hate you."

"I was going to replace it," I laughed. "And as for the fondling... well, could you blame me?"

"We made margaritas!" Susie sung as she and Nora walked out to the patio with a pitcher of margaritas and a tray of sandwiches.

"You're the best, baby." Ethan stood and planted a kiss on Susie's cheek.

I got up and helped Nora pour the drinks, and then grabbed a sandwich. "Thanks, baby," I said quietly, before mimicking Ethan's gesture and kissing her on the cheek.

"Any time," she smiled.

Our brief exchange didn't go unnoticed by our friends. "AWW! Look at you two," Susie crooned. "A-friggen-dorable!"

We ate, drank, and lounged by the pool for a while. Eventually we decided to set up the volleyball net in the pool and play a game, Nora and me versus Susie and Ethan. We played around in the pool, volleying the ball back and forth, and hoisted the girls on our shoulders until we were laughing so hard we could barely stand. Then Ethan and I played a few rounds one on one, trying to show off for the girls while they feigned interest from the sidelines.

"Okay, that's it," Ethan said, trying to catch his breath. "Let's just call it a draw, dude."

"Yeah, I'll grab some beers," I said, equally exhausted.

The combination of the alcohol and the hot sun had us all a little buzzed, and it wasn't long before I pulled Nora into the lounge chair with me. I rested my hands on her hips and nuzzled in her neck, inhaling her sugary scent and brushing occasional kisses against her skin.

"Get a room, you two," Ethan teased. "You're just as bad as you were in high school!"

"Get used to it!" I said, unapologetically.

That night we all decided to go out for drinks at The Landing. It was karaoke night, so by the time we got there the bar was already full of people.

"So, Nora, are you gonna get up there and show all these idiots how it's done?" Susie said, motioning to the stage where some guy was butchering "Sweet Home Alabama."

"I don't think so," Nora said. "It's packed in here and I'm not nearly drunk enough to embarrass myself in front of all these people."

"Well, let's see if we can change that," Ethan said, getting up from the table. "First round is on me!"

We were well into our second round of drinks when I caught sight of Lindsey approaching our table. I tensed up immediately, bracing myself for whatever trouble she would inevitably start.

"Hey guys," she said, stopping in front of our table. "Isn't this just the cutest thing. You've got the old gang back together!" Her mocking tone wasn't lost on anyone, and her comment was met with awkward silence.

"What's up, Linds?" Ethan said, breaking the tension.

"Not much," Lindsey responded, leaning her elbows on the table so we got an eyeful of the cleavage she had propped up on display. "Just waiting for my turn up on stage."

"Oh, I didn't know you sang," Nora politely remarked.

"What, you thought you were the only one around here who could?" Lindsey snapped, glaring at Nora.

"Easy," Ethan said firmly, warning Lindsey to back off.

I squeezed Nora's leg reassuringly. I wanted to do something to defend her and put Lindsey in her place, but I knew it would only make things worse. Lindsey was relentless, and for about the millionth time I wished that I hadn't been stupid enough to get involved with her.

"I better head up there. Enjoy your evening!" Lindsey said sarcastically, flipping her blonde hair and sauntering toward the stage.

We sat there in stunned silence for a moment before Susie piped in. "Now that's one branch of your family tree that I really wish I could saw off," she said, looking to Ethan.

"Amen to that!" Ethan said as we all laughed.

"I think it's time for another round." I got up from the table and made my way over to the bar. I figured we all needed something a little stronger, so I ordered a round of shots in addition to our drinks. As I was paying the bartender, I felt someone press up against me and turned to see that it was Lindsey.

"What do you want, Lindsey?" I grumbled, not bothering to hide my irritation.

"Jeez, baby, so serious," she said, stroking her hand over my chest. "Just wanted to remind you what you're missing."

She winked, turning toward the stage before I had a chance to push her away.

When I returned to the table with our drinks, Lindsey was getting up on the small stage with the microphone. The first notes of the song began to play as I sat down, and when I realized what song she was singing, I cringed.

Lindsey started belting out the first verse of "Don't Cha" by the Pussycat Dolls, while shaking her hips and dancing provocatively. She wasn't a terrible singer, but to me she just looked ridiculous.

"Well, she's definitely not subtle," Nora stated matter-of-factly.

"Girl does NOT know when to give up!" Susie said, laughing.

Ethan shot me a sympathetic look from across the table. I was totally screwed. I meant to tell Nora about Lindsey, but I could never figure out how to bring it up. Now it was going to seem like I was hiding it, and Nora absolutely hated dishonestly.

Fuck.

"Nora, you've got to put that girl in her place," Susie said. "Just get up there! It will be fun, and you're a thousand times better than that little skank."

"Okay, fine," Nora finally agreed. "But I'm going to need some liquid courage!"

She threw back her shot, followed by Susie's, before walking over to the stage and talking to the guy in charge. As soon as Lindsey was finished, it was Nora's turn. Susie, Ethan and I got up to stand closer to the stage to cheer her on, while a surprised Lindsey stood off to the side to watch.

I knew that Nora was nervous, but the shots must have helped because she didn't look it. She was wearing a white tank top with short denim shorts and cowboy boots. Damn, she was fucking sexy.

She sang "Mama's Broken Heart" by Miranda Lambert, and the crowd absolutely loved it. Her voice was incredible, and she worked the stage like a pro, but I had a hard time paying attention to anything except for the wiggling of her hips and her long, tanned legs in those sexy shorts and boots.

chapter seven

Nora

The crowd roared as I got off the stage, and when I looked over and saw the bitchy look on Lindsey's face, I was satisfied that she had officially been put in her place. I wasn't usually so competitive, but that girl was on my last nerve. Either way, I'd had fun on stage so it was worth it.

I saw Jake walking toward me through the crowd, but before I could reach him, Lindsey blocked my path.

"You're awfully feisty tonight," she said, getting right in my face.

"I'm not trying to fight with you, Lindsey," I said, stepping away from her. "I just don't understand why you keep going after Jake when he's obviously not interested."

"He was certainly interested the last time we were here," she said. "When he took me home and had his hands all over me. He couldn't get enough. Right, Jake?"

She glanced back at Jake, who stood frozen as all the color drained from his face. "He's a real animal in the sack," she smirked. "I don't blame you for wanting him all to yourself."

My stomach dropped. That couldn't be true. He couldn't have been with her, of all people.

"Jake?" I looked up at him, waiting for him to deny what she was saying. But he didn't. I felt like throwing up, and I could feel the bile rising in my throat. I had to get out of here.

"Nora, wait ..."

I didn't turn around when I heard him. I stormed out of the bar and kept walking. My eyes were welling up with tears, and I could barely see where I was going. I didn't care. All I wanted was to get away from them. Fortunately, it was late enough that it was almost empty in the park, so I sat down on a bench swing and tried to collect my thoughts.

Was I overreacting? It's not as though I'd thought Jake had given up women for four years. Okay, maybe a part of me hoped that he had been pining over me and had been as miserable as I was, but I was mostly upset that it was Lindsey he had been with.

Lindsey.

She was awful, and he knew how much I detested her and her ruthless attempts to "steal" him from me when we were in high school. I hated the fact that she had gotten him. And let's face it; I *really* detested the fact that she'd been intimate with him when I hadn't. As close as Jake and I were, she had a part of him that I didn't.

It wasn't long before I noticed Jake approaching out of the corner of my eye. I didn't look up at him when he sat down on the other side of the bench.

"Shit, Nora. I'm so sorry," he said. "I should have told you. I meant to, I–I just didn't know how to, and it's not something I'm proud of. She found me at a weak moment when I was obliterated drunk. Not that it's any excuse. I was just stupid, and I should have known better. I'm *so* damn sorry."

I softened a little bit at his words and the pained expression on his face, but it still hurt. I knew I was probably overreacting. He hadn't *really* done anything wrong since we hadn't been together then, but I couldn't help being jealous. When I thought about the two of them together, pain and anger ripped through me and tore me apart. My feelings for him were stronger than I thought they were, and that scared me a little bit too.

"Do you… did you have feelings for her?" I stammered, still not looking at him.

"No. Not now and not ever. I swear. You are the only girl I've ever truly had feelings for, and I'm not just saying that. When you left, I was miserable for a long, long time. I couldn't get you out of my head no matter how much time passed, and there were times when I was in a pretty dark place. Lindsey was a stupid mistake that I regretted instantly. She means nothing to me. She never did, and she never will." He reached over and gently pulled my chin toward him so I would meet his gaze. "You mean everything to me."

I let him take my hand and weave his fingers through mine. "Just the thought of you being with her… it makes me crazy," I said. "When I lost you, I was completely broken. I never once let anyone else get close to me, and I guess I wanted to believe that you were just as broken as I was."

"Baby, I *was* broken. I was completely shattered! There was not a single day that went by that I didn't think of you. I've been yours since the day we met. Yours, and only yours. The stupid thing with Lindsey never changed that for a second. You own me, Nora."

The pain of his confession still stung, but the warmth of his words was slowly surpassing it. He seemed so genuine. It was impossible to stay angry at him.

"I'm sorry for being so dramatic," I said, wiping the tears from my face. "It's not really my business anyway. I wasn't even here. I'm just being stupid."

He slid closer to me and put his arm around me. "It is definitely your business," he said, pulling me in to him. "And I'm glad you're jealous, it shows me that you care. Besides, this is nothing; in high school, I used to pick a fight with any guy who looked at you for too long, remember?"

I laughed. "Yeah, and I used to pretend to get so mad even

though I secretly thought it was kinda hot. There were definitely a few girls that I almost threw down with when they came on to you. I guess we've always run a little hot and cold, eh?"

"I think it just means we're passionate. Nothing wrong with that," he said as he leaned over and kissed me gently on the lips. "As long as we trust each other, we'll be okay."

After Jake walked me to my front door, he gave me a sweet kiss that I deepened by clasping my arms around his neck and molding my body to his. He pressed me against the door, and I reached behind me with one hand to open it.

"Upstairs," I said breathlessly. I didn't want the night to end yet, and I needed to clear the images of him and Lindsey from my head. The alcohol in my system had me feeling bold, and I wanted Jake. Now.

He lifted me up before we stumbled inside, and I wrapped my legs around his waist, holding on tightly as he carried me effortlessly up the stairs and into my bedroom, where we fell on top of my bed. I grabbed the hem of his shirt, trying to pull it off, and when he sat up to take it off the rest of the way, I ripped my tank top over my head and unclasped my bra, throwing them both to the side. He looked down at me, his eyes dark and full of desire.

"God, you're beautiful," he said, lowering himself over me and covering my mouth with his.

Each touch set me on fire, and I ached for him. I undid my shorts and wiggled out of them, desperate to feel more of him. I grabbed his hips, crying out in pleasure when he rubbed against me through the thin material of my panties. Still, I wanted more. With shaky fingers I reached between us and unbuttoned his jeans. As I pulled the zipper down, my fingers grazed his hard length, and the resulting groan that came from him sent me into overdrive. I pushed his jeans down as far as I could and let him kick them the rest of the way off.

"God, baby, I want you so bad." His voice was husky and deep with desire as he settled between my legs and rocked against me, his firm arousal pressing exactly where I needed him. As his lips came down on mine, I moaned into his mouth and nipped at his bottom lip. With only two thin layers of fabric separating us, the sensation was driving me wild, and I was desperate for more. I moved my hand to the waistband of his boxers and started to pull them down, eager to keep going, but he grabbed my hand to stop me.

"Not now, baby."

Confused, I stopped and looked up at him. "Why not?"

He lifted himself from me and began to stand up. "Because you're too special to me."

"Ugh!" I wailed, not bothering to hide my frustration. "I don't want to be special. I want you inside me!"

As soon as the words escaped my lips, Jake was back on top of me, pressing me into the mattress as he kissed me wildly. His hand trailed down my body and into my panties, where I was aching for his touch.

"You're so wet," he growled as he began slowly rubbing his fingers along my center.

"I want you," I practically begged.

He slipped a finger inside me, and I could feel the pleasure building. I was already so close. I gripped him tightly as he continued to move in and out of me, and it wasn't long before I cried out as he sent me over the edge.

Jake shifted to his side, still holding me, and brushed his lips against mine. I let my breathing return to normal and wondered why he wasn't taking this where I wanted it to go.

"That's not exactly what I meant," I whispered, avoiding his eyes. "Why… why didn't you want to…?"

He took me by the chin, forcing me to meet his gaze. "Nora, trust me. I want to. I want to so fucking bad, it hurts. Literally." He motioned to his still rock hard erection. "But not like this. Not when we're both drunk, and we've been fighting."

"Okay, so why not before? When we were in high school? There were more than enough opportunities then when I tried to give myself to you, but you refused. You'd been with loads of other girls, but you never wanted me!" I hadn't meant to get so upset, but I'd had it bottled up for so long that it just came pouring out.

"That's what you think?"

"What else am I supposed to think?" I asked. "All those girls in high school, even stupid Lindsey, why is it different with me?"

"Nora," he said, tenderly stroking my cheek with his fingertips. "It's different with you because I actually care about you. I've never been with someone who I care about. It was always just meaningless sex. When there are no feelings involved, it's simple, but when you really care about someone, like I do for you, it's a total game changer. It means everything. That's uncharted territory for me, and to be honest, it scares the shit out of me. I've never had to worry about what happens afterwards, but with you, it's completely different." He stared down at me, his blue eyes piercing into mine. "If you do what you've always done, then you'll get what you've always got, and I don't want just a one-time thing with you. I don't want to ever let you go."

"Really? It wasn't because you didn't want to be with someone who'd never done it before?"

"Yes, really." He kissed me softly. "It had nothing to do with the fact that you were a virgin. How could you think that? I mean, even now..." Jake stopped suddenly, and I could see the wheels in his head turning. "Nora, when you said earlier that you had never let anyone else get close to you, did you mean that you were never... with... anyone? Are you still...?"

A blush instantly rose to my cheeks, and I looked down, trying to hide my face from him. I didn't want him to know that at twenty-two years old, I was still a virgin. It was too embarrassing.

"Nora?" I could feel his questioning gaze bearing into me. "You aren't... are you?"

"Um, well..."

"You're still a virgin?" His eyes lit up, and a smile played at the corners of his mouth.

"Well, yeah. I mean, I was really busy, and I just..." Before I could finish stammering through my explanation, his mouth was on mine.

"That's seriously the best news I've ever heard," he said, a ridiculously huge smile on his face. "The idea that some other guy had you, when it was supposed to be me. . . it was driving me crazy! I wanted to be your first, and your last. Why were so ashamed to tell me?"

"I didn't want you to think I was all innocent and inexperienced."

"Baby, I've never thought of you as innocent, and you sure as hell aren't inexperienced. You've always been able to drive me crazy and turn me on like nobody else. You know exactly where to touch me and how to make me wild. There's nothing inexperienced about you. I'm happy as hell that I'm the one who gets to experience you."

Jake

Nora was working at her father's office for the next couple of days, and I was busy putting the finishing touches on the cabin. Even though we didn't see each other, we still spoke daily on the phone and through text messages. I was amazed at how much I loved even that. We could talk about nothing at all, and it was the best part of my day.

The one thing I hadn't mentioned to her yet was my interview. I had a meeting with the head of an architectural firm about a big project they had planned in Charleston, and if by some miracle they actually hired me, it would mean relocating there for several months. It was only an hour or two away, but telling Nora would mean opening the door for a conversation about the future, and I wasn't ready to go there with her yet. Not because I had doubts about wanting a future with Nora—there wasn't a doubt in my mind—but I still didn't know where she stood. She was due to return to New York for law school in the fall, and she'd given me no indication that her plans had changed.

Even though she was still furious at her parents for lying to her, it didn't change the fact that, deep down, she was desperate to please them. Since she was a little girl, she'd been putting her own happiness aside in order to make her parents happy. Dating me was the one thing she'd done on her own, and we saw how that turned out. Nora was strong, stubborn and confident in every aspect of her life, but her weakness was her parents.

As much as I wanted to tell her to make her own decisions and do what made her happy, I stayed out of it. It was a sensitive issue for Nora, and if she were going to stand up to her parents, it would have to be *her* decision. The last thing she needed was yet another person telling her what to do. I'd made that mistake once before, the summer after she graduated high school when I told her that she should be going to school for music. I couldn't stand watching her throw away her dreams, and I knew she could have a real future in it. She was an amazing singer and songwriter, and I knew it was what she truly wanted to do, so I opened my big mouth. Unfortunately it had resulted in a big fight between us, so I'd learned my lesson.

Now, Nora and I seemed to avoid talking about the future entirely, almost as though it was an unspoken agreement between us. We couldn't dodge it forever. Sooner or later we were going to have to talk about it. That conversation could lead to me getting everything I've wanted since I was eighteen, or I could end up losing her forever. I wasn't ready to risk losing her yet. She was still skittish, and I needed more time to make her realize that we were meant to be together.

I'd always loved Charleston. It was so rich in history, and walking down the cobblestone streets with horse and carriages at every turn, it was like stepping into another time. That was one of the reasons I was so anxious to be a part of this project. It was a full renovation of a historic home downtown, and the idea was to incorporate the old design into the new design. It would be classic and historic, but with a modern feel. It was exactly the kind of project I'd always wanted to do.

My dad had done some construction work with the one of the guys from the firm who was in charge of the project, so he'd been able to pull some strings to get me the interview. This firm oversaw a ton of architectural projects throughout the state, so if they hired me for this project and liked my work, it would mean other future projects as well.

I thought my meeting had gone pretty well, but I wouldn't find out for a few weeks. The guy I met with, Jason Tredwell, seemed to like the ideas I had, but he was surprised when I told him that this would be my first official project. It was a long shot that he would actually hire me when there were so many other more experienced architects in the running. If I didn't get this job, I would have to start looking at firms farther away, which would make it almost impossible for me to stay in Beaufort.

After the meeting, I spent some time walking around downtown before driving back home. It had been a long time since I'd been in Charleston, but it hadn't changed much since then. My first time visiting had been with Nora. Her grandmother owned a house there, and when Nora spent time there over the summer, I would come to see her. She'd shown me all around Charleston and took me to some of the small surrounding beach towns. Some of my best memories with Nora were from time that we spent there.

It was late afternoon, and I was stopped at a gas station just outside of Beaufort when I got a text message from Nora.

Still on for tmw?

I smiled and quickly typed a response.

You bet! How's ur day goin?

A few minutes later, my phone chimed with another message.

Not too bad. Long day at the office. Can't wait for tmw…
Me either. Miss u…call me ltr?
If ur lucky ;)

I chuckled at her last message and put my phone away before climbing back into my truck. Just a few text messages from her, and I was already in a better mood. Now, instead of stressing over whether or not I would get the Charleston project, I could spend the rest of my day planning out the details for my date with Nora tomorrow. I still felt awful about what happened with Lindsey, and even though it had ended up bringing us closer, I was determined to make our date tomorrow extra special… and drama-free.

After a quick stop at the cabin to make sure everything was in order, I drove the rest of the way home with a smile on my face and started counting down the hours until I would see my girl again.

chapter eight

Nora

As usual, I had no idea what Jake was planning for the day, but this time he did tell me to pack a bathing suit and a change of clothes. I was beyond curious about what he had planned for us. By noon, I was dressed and ready, even though he wasn't picking me up for another hour. We hadn't been able to see each other for the past few days, and I was surprised at how much I'd missed him and how anxious I was to see him again. I would have thought that after missing him for four years, a couple of days would seem like nothing. Instead, it only made me crave more time with him. Had it been like this the first time around? We'd been inseparable in high school, so I supposed we didn't have too many opportunities to miss each other back then.

In an attempt to settle my nerves and help pass the time, I grabbed my guitar and went out on the front porch to play. For the first time in four years, I'd actually started writing a new song. It was just bits and pieces, and it wasn't like anyone would ever hear it, but it helped me unscramble my thoughts and make sense of what I was feeling. Since I never played or wrote anything while I was away at school, I had forgotten how much it helped to put my thoughts into music. No wonder I'd been so confused all the time.

For me, music was an essential element of life. As dramatic as it sounded, it was true. When I was growing up, and even now, I couldn't talk back to my parents or disagree with them. So, instead of yelling and screaming, I would go upstairs and write a song. It was the only way I could let my emotions out. Without music, I probably would've exploded from keeping things bottled up. Even though I wouldn't be able to make a career with music, I knew I had to find a way to incorporate it into my life as a lawyer. Somehow.

I looked up when I heard Jake's truck coming down the driveway. He hopped out and met me with a big hug that lifted me off the ground.

"Hey, you!" I said, laughing at his enthusiastic greeting.

"Hey, yourself." He lowered me to the ground and leaned down to give me a quick kiss. "Did you remember to pack a bag like I told you to?"

"Yes. Are you finally going to tell me where you're taking me?" Jake had told me to pack for an overnight and bring my bathing suit, but he hadn't told me where we were going or what we'd be doing.

"You'll find out soon enough," he said with a grin.

He convinced me to bring my guitar along, which was a little nerve-wracking, but I loved playing for Jake. Most of the time, I sang songs from the artists we both liked, and he would just lie back and close his eyes, or sometimes sing along. It was comforting, and I'd missed it.

Jake helped me carry my bag and guitar down to the truck and put them in the back. Once we were both settled, he held up a red bandana.

"Will you put this on to cover your eyes?" he asked.

"Huh? Why?"

"I want it to be a surprise."

"Okay, but if I end up in some dark dungeon, I'm going to be really pissed."

"That's for our next date," he joked as he tied the bandana

around my eyes.

Once I was sufficiently blinded, Jake started driving. I tried to imagine where he could possibly be taking me. After a little while, I felt him pull onto a dirt road, and a few minutes later he stopped, shut off the engine, and helped me out. I held tightly onto his arm as he carefully led me to wherever we were going.

"Okay, you can look now," he said when we stopped walking.

I pulled the bandana off, and when I realized what I was looking at, I was completely stunned. We were at his grandfather's old fishing cabin, but it was nothing like the old, dilapidated shack that I remembered.

"Oh my God, Jake! Did you do this?"

"Yeah," he answered with a grin. "I started working on it a few months ago."

"It's absolutely amazing!" He had completely transformed the old shack into a beautiful cabin. It wasn't anything too flashy or modern; it was rustic and blended perfectly into the surroundings. I turned to him in amazement. "I can't believe you did this. It's incredible."

He led me up the steps and opened the door to let me inside. When I saw what he had done there, I was speechless. It was nothing like the desolate interior that I remembered from before. Instead, it was like walking into an actual home that could be lived in. It was cozy, welcoming and had everything anyone would need.

"I can't believe this is the same place," I said.

"Do you like it?"

"Are you kidding?" I turned to him in disbelief. "I absolutely love it!"

"I haven't spent much time here over the last few years," he said, leaning up against the wall. "But when I got my degree in architecture, my grandpa finally agreed to let me renovate."

"You did a beautiful job. You're so talented, Jake."

He shrugged. "I really love doing this kind of thing, and I had so many great memories here. I was glad to be able to give something back." He took a step toward me and brushed his fingers along my cheek. "I thought so much about you while I was working on it, even before you came back. All my best memories here are from when I was with you. You're everywhere. That's why I wanted you to see it first. You're a part of this place."

I could feel my eyes filling with tears. Before I had a chance to say anything, his lips were on mine in a tender kiss.

"Thank you for letting me be part of this," I said, pressing my forehead against his.

He took my by the hand again, leading me across the room. "I almost forgot to show you the best part." He opened a narrow door off to the side. "Ta da! A fully functioning toilet. Remember the old outhouse in the woods that you refused to use?"

"Ugh! Don't remind me, I hated that awful thing. I used to avoid drinking any liquids just so I wouldn't have to use it!"

He laughed. "Well, now you never have to. The shower is still outside, but don't worry, it's nice."

Once he finished showing me all the amazing things he'd done, he led me back outside and grabbed my guitar and a picnic basket from the back of his truck. We walked down to the dock where his grandfather's old rowboat was tied up alongside, floating peacefully in the still water.

"Feel like going for a little boat ride?" Jake asked, his blue eyes twinkling.

He climbed into the boat with the basket in hand and tucked my guitar case safely under the seat before turning to help me in. As I settled into the seat at the back of the small boat, I watched as Jake untied it and gently pushed off the dock before grabbing the oars. When he started rowing, I couldn't help but stare at his biceps flexing against his white t-shirt as he pulled the oars against the glassy water in perfect unison. While he rowed us along smoothly, I leaned back and enjoyed the feel of the sun radiating down on me. Reaching one hand over the side of the boat, I dipped my fingers into the water and watched them skim over the smooth surface.

We approached the grassy shore on the other side, and Jake hopped out to pull the boat up. After helping me climb out, he grabbed the picnic basket and led me into a grassy field that I remembered coming to with him before. It was a gorgeous meadow right on the water, surrounded by live oaks and old farm fields. Butterflies fluttered around patches of flowers among the green grass, and the sky was bright blue with the occasional white, puffy cloud rolling by.

Jake set down the picnic basket, pulled out a blanket and laid it on the grass. He started unpacking the basket, taking out a bottle of white wine, cheese, crackers, and containers of what looked like homemade chicken salad.

"Wow, I'm impressed," I said as I sat down, adjusting my red dress over my legs. "That looks a lot like one of your mom's famous picnic lunches."

"Busted," he grinned. "I was going to try and do it myself, but when I told my mom it was for you, she insisted on taking control. Apparently she didn't think my cooking was good enough for you."

"Well, I happen to love your mom's cooking, so I can't say that I'm disappointed. In fact, I'll have to stop by for a visit so I can thank her for saving me from your culinary creations."

"She would love that, but she probably wouldn't let you leave. She's missed you, too."

I helped him divide the food onto two paper plates and grabbed the plastic silverware from a side pocket on the picnic basket. Jake opened the wine and poured it into paper cups, handing one to me.

The food that Jake's mother made was delicious, and it wasn't long before we'd finished almost all of it. It was the perfect day, sunny but not swelteringly hot, and I couldn't think of any place I'd rather be. We sat around and talked for a long time, and after a few more cups of wine, I decided to grab my guitar from the boat.

When I returned with my guitar, Jake was lounging comfortably on his back with his arms tucked behind his head. He watched me silently as I took my guitar out of the case and positioned it easily in my lap. I started strumming softly, not playing anything in particular, and eventually morphed into a couple songs – a little Rascal Flatts, some Lady Antebellum, and of course, Miranda Lambert.

Jake had closed his eyes to listen, and after a while I was pretty sure he'd dozed off. When I put my guitar down, he extended his arm out to the side for me to lie down next to him. I rested my head on his shoulder and cuddled into him when he pulled me close. It was the most content I'd felt in a long time. As I watched the clouds float overhead, it wasn't long before I drifted off as well.

A drop of water landed on my cheek, waking me up and interrupting my moment of tranquility. When I opened my eyes, I saw that the blue sky had turned gray and mean with the promise of a summer storm. This was a common occurrence around here. Short summer storms would come through on even the most beautiful of days.

"Jake, wake up!" I nudged his arm and started packing up the last remnants of our picnic before everything got soaked. He opened his eyes groggily, jumping into motion when he saw the clouds overhead threatening to dump rain all over us.

We moved quickly across the water, thanks to his speedy rowing, and were only a few yards away from the dock when the sky opened up and rain started hammering down on us. I shrieked, making a pathetic attempt to cover myself with the cardigan I was holding, while Jake just watched me and laughed.

When we edged up against the dock I practically leapt out of the boat and carried my guitar and the picnic basket back to the shelter of the cabin. I was about to go inside to get away from the storm, but when I looked for Jake, I saw that he was still out on the dock. He was leisurely tying up the rowboat and securing it to the dock, clearly in no hurry despite the buckets of rain coming down over his head.

"What's taking so long?" I said, rushing to the end of the dock where he was still standing. "In case you didn't notice, we're getting drenched!"

Jake just smiled. "Since when do you care about getting a little wet? The Nora I remember used to love running around in summer storms." He strode over to where I stood, stopping only inches from me, and slid his hands up my arms. "It's kinda nice, isn't it?"

I nodded and stepped closer, looking up at him through the sheets of rain. He was gorgeous. Especially when he was dripping wet. I reached up and traced his jawline, trailing my finger through the droplets of rain that covered his skin, and watched as his eyes turned dark with desire.

Within a half a second his mouth was on mine and his hands were at my hips drawing me closer. His kiss started off slow, but when his tongue met mine, it became needy and impassioned. I slowly ran my hands up his hard chest and over his shoulders, pulling myself closer to him. His grip around me tightened, and he moved his hands down, grabbing my bottom and lifting me up. I wound my legs around his waist, firmly holding myself to him.

"I want you," he mumbled against my lips. "I can't wait any longer."

"I want you too, Jake."

My lips explored his neck, placing kisses along his throat and nibbling his earlobe. He let out a groan and started walking even faster up the stairs to the cabin. When we reached the door, he pressed my back against it as his hands found their way underneath my dress and he caressed my bare skin, his fingers only inches away from where I wanted them to be.

"I've wanted this for so long, Nora."

"You have no idea," I whispered against his ear, driving him into a frenzy.

He pushed open the cabin door, kicking it closed behind him. I unwrapped my legs from his waist, and he gently lowered me until my feet were back on the ground. Our clothes were soaking wet from the rain, clinging to our skin, and I wanted to eliminate the layers between us and feel his bare skin on mine. My hands dropped to his waist, grasping the bottom of his shirt and peeling it off him.

Jake's hands moved over me slowly, warming my damp skin and sending my body into a fever. With shaky hands, I reached for the waistband of his jeans and unfastened the button. As I gradually lowered the metal zipper, I stroked my fingers along the hardness of his arousal that was pressing against it, causing him to growl in pleasure. In one swift motion, he grasped the hem of my dress and yanked it over my head, tossing it to the side as we made our way over to the bed.

I tugged his jeans the rest of the way down to the floor, and with one hand he reached around to unclasp my bra and pull it off me. Gently he lowered me onto the mattress, hovering above me as his mouth moved down my neck and along my collarbone. He cupped my breasts, caressing his thumbs over the hard peaks of my nipples, and the contact sent shockwaves through my body. When he drew my nipple into his mouth, teasing and sucking it with his tongue, I cried out shamelessly, clawing at his back with my fingers.

"God, baby, I want to be inside you so bad," he choked out as he trailed his hand down my stomach, grasping the waistband of my panties and sliding them down my legs. "I don't want to hurt you though, so I'm gonna try and take this slow."

He knelt between my legs and pressed his lips to my inner thigh, tenderly kissing his way to my aching center. As soon as his tongue flicked my sensitive flesh, I arched into him as pure desire shot through me.

"I love the way you taste, Nora."

Gripping my thighs, he increased the pressure of his mouth and continued to lick and suck until I was practically panting and begging for release. Reaching down, I grabbed fistfuls of his hair in my hands, desperately pulling him closer. He growled against me hungrily, speeding up his exquisite assault, sending me over the edge as I screamed out in pleasure.

As the waves of my orgasm rolled through me, Jake reached into the pocket of his jeans and pulled out a condom from his wallet. I watched, transfixed, as he tore open the packet and shed his boxers, rolling it onto his impressive length before moving back onto the bed. He positioned himself above me, and I saw a look of hesitation cross his face.

My hands clutched the firm muscles of his back, and I tilted my mouth up, kissing along his neck until I reached his ear. "I need you, Jake," I whispered.

His body shuddered slightly, and he moaned, letting his hips fall between my legs. I could feel him pressing against my entrance, teasing me. Very slowly he began to ease inside me, and my body tensed slightly, expecting pain, but it was nothing like I thought it would be. Although I felt some discomfort as I stretched to accommodate his size, it was masked by the pleasure I felt, concealed by the throbbing desire to feel him inside me.

"Tell me if I hurt you." His voice was rough and unsteady, like he was fighting to maintain control. Once he was all the way inside he stilled, giving me a chance to get used to the sensation of him filling me.

"Don't stop…"

Cautiously he began to move, and the sensation was overwhelming. After a few moments, any lingering pain was gone, replaced with currents of pleasure surging through me.

"You feel incredible," he groaned, kissing my neck as he

moved inside me. "You're so damn tight, baby. So perfect."

I began to shift my hips against his, urging him to go faster. He responded immediately, picking up speed and causing me to cry out as my body began to climb. Gripping his back tightly, I lifted my hips, meeting him thrust for thrust until my insides coiled around him, and I screamed out his name as my release tore through me. Jake rocked into me a few more times, driving deep inside before he stilled, groaning loudly with his own release.

Neither of us moved for what felt like several minutes as we lay there and caught our breath. Finally, Jake leaned down, tenderly brushing his lips against mine.

"Holy shit. That was… wow." He pulled out of me gently and rolled onto his side, gathering me tightly against him. "Are you okay?" He nuzzled into my neck.

"I've never been better," I smiled, dropping a kiss to his chest.

We lay there in silence, wrapped around each other as the rain pounded on the roof above us. I'd never felt such complete bliss before, and I savored the feeling as I eventually drifted into a peaceful sleep.

Jake

The sun was barely up when I woke to Nora's soft kisses on my chest. She was still wrapped up in my arms, and I ran my hand down the silky smooth skin of her spine, remembering how amazing she'd felt last night. Being with her was unlike anything I'd ever experienced before, and I was already craving her again, even though it had only been a few hours. I didn't think I'd ever get enough of her.

As if she could read my mind, Nora continued her trail of

kisses up my neck, and I groaned when she rubbed her body against my morning wood, which was getting harder by the second.

"Good morning, Mr. Harris." She smiled at me deviously. "Glad to see you're... up."

"Aren't you hungry?" I asked, even though it was the last thing on my mind when she was pressing up against me. Her hair was mussed up and sexy, and her just-woke-up voice had a raspy tone that was nothing short of seductive.

"Not for food."

She reached down, grabbing my hard on, and began moving her soft hand up and down its length. With each stroke, my need for her intensified, until I couldn't wait another second before burying myself deep inside her. With one hand I reached over the side of the bed, fumbling around until I located the jeans that I had discarded the night before, and hastily dug a condom from the pocket.

Nora took the foil packet from my hand and ripped it open with her teeth before slowly and tortuously rolling it over my eager cock. With an eager growl I rolled on top of her, crushing my mouth to hers and giving in to what we both desperately craved.

Nope. I definitely would never be able to get enough of her.

Once we had satisfied our hunger for each other, a low rumble from my stomach reminded me how starving I was for actual food. As much as I wanted to spend the rest of the day entwined with Nora, it had been a long time since we'd eaten, so I reluctantly climbed out of bed and threw on some clothes.

I hopped in my truck and made the short drive to the nearest bakery to grab us something to eat. As I perused the cases of various bagels, muffins and croissants, I realized that I had no idea what Nora liked for breakfast. Since we'd never woken up together before today, it was the one meal we'd never shared. I ordered two coffees and a large assortment of baked goods, while also making a mental note to find out what Nora's favorite breakfast foods were. If I had it my way, we would be spending a lot of mornings together from this point forward.

The storm was long gone, leaving us with another gorgeous, hot, sunny day. When I got back to the cabin with our food and brought it inside, Nora was nowhere to be found. After a split second of panic, I looked out the window and saw that she had changed into her bikini and was lying out at the end of the dock. I quickly threw on my swim trunks and went outside to join her, grabbing our food on the way out.

After we had finished eating, I spread my towel out alongside hers and lay down next to her. There wasn't a cloud in the sky, and the sun was beating down on us, warming my skin and relaxing my whole body, making me feel like I didn't have a care in the world. It was too hot to do anything else, and I couldn't think of anywhere else I'd rather be. Or anyone else I'd rather be with.

When I couldn't take the heat anymore, I stood up and dove into the cool water below. It wasn't that cold, but it sure as hell was refreshing, and I swam around until I no longer felt like my insides were going to boil.

Nora had turned onto her stomach and was watching me as I swam over to her.

"Wanna come in?" I asked, lifting myself up on the edge of the dock so I was facing her. "It's reaaal nice!"

"Nah, I think I'll stay up here," she said, rolling over again so she was on her back.

"If you say so…" I climbed the rest of the way up, and before she had a chance to say anything, I was lying on top of her, dripping wet.

"Jake!" she shrieked, flopping around underneath me.

"Aw, come on, feels nice doesn't it?" Propping myself up on

my elbows I shook my hair, spraying droplets of water all over her face.

"You're such an ass!" she laughed, swatting me on the arm.

She shifted beneath me, and the movement of her warm, bare skin against mine was enough to send desire shooting through me.

I'm like a horny friggin' teenager over here!

I rolled off her, reminding myself that it had been Nora's first (and second) time, so she was probably a little sore.

"So…" I said, looking over at her. "How are you today? I didn't hurt you, did I?"

She blushed and shy smile crept across her face. "No, you definitely didn't hurt me. I'm a little sore, but in a good way."

I trailed my fingers along her smooth stomach and heard her sharp intake of breath. "So… how was it?"

Her smile got bigger. "It was great. Perfect, actually, and now that I know what I've been missing out on, I'm definitely going to want to keep doing it. Think you might be up for that?"

"Oh, I am most definitely up for that." I leaned over to kiss her, but when I pulled back her expression had changed.

"So, um…" she began nervously. "Was it… okay for you?"

I drew her close to me and looked right into her beautiful green eyes. "Nora, it was amazing. Hands down, the best night of my entire life. It was a first for me too, because I never knew it could be like that. Okay, baby?"

She nodded, but before she could say anything else her phone rang. Looking at the screen she groaned, hitting the ignore button and putting it back down.

"Who was that?"

"My parents," she answered, the aggravation clear in her voice. "They're coming home today."

"Have you talked to them at all?"

"Not since I found out what they did." She let out a deep breath. "I'm so mad I don't even know what to say to them. I've never confronted them about anything like this before. They just don't understand."

"Well, maybe you don't have to…"

"No, I do. I can't avoid them forever."

We spent the rest of the day out in the sun, relaxing and goofing around with each other. When it was time to drive Nora home, I was glad to see that her parents hadn't arrived yet. This was going to be complicated enough, and if they saw me it would only add fuel to the fire. I dropped her off, giving her a kiss and wishing her luck before she walked inside and prepared for whatever kind of shitstorm her parents might bring.

That evening, Ethan met me at my apartment with a six-pack in hand. We hung out, drank beers and played some video games, and I had to give him props because he waited a whole hour and a half before asking me about Nora.

"So, how's things going with you two?" he said, trying to act nonchalant.

"Good," I replied without going into detail.

"Did you finally… ya know…"

"Aw, come on man! That's none of your damn business. Since when did you get so nosy?"

"Sorry, dude, can't blame me for being curious," he said. "I guess I'll just have to wait until Susie tells me. You know how those gals love to gossip about us."

"Okay," I laughed. "But I want it on record that I kept my mouth shut about it."

"Seriously though, how's it going with you two?"

I leaned back on the couch, taking a long pull from my beer. "It's pretty great. You know how I feel about Nora, she's amazing. But there's a lot of shit we'll have to figure out eventually, so I'm trying not to scare her off. Then again, her parents came home to-day so I'm sure they'll find a way to do it for me."

"I'm sure you two will work it out," he assured me. "Nora's parents are pretty controlling, but she's not a little kid anymore. Have you talked to her since they got back?"

"Not yet. I figured I ought to give her some space to talk things out with them. I don't want to make it worse." I got up and went to the kitchen to grab two more beers, and when I sat back down, Ethan's phone beeped to alert him of a text message.

"It's Susie," he said, looking at his phone. "She said Nora is crashing at our place tonight, so it must not have gone well with her folks."

Immediately I pulled out my phone and texted Nora.
How'd it go? R u ok?

A few seconds later she sent me a message back.
Not 2 good...I'll fill u in later. Stayin w/ Sus for a bit. Needed 2 get away from them.

I hated that she had to go through this. My parents were nothing like hers, so I couldn't even imagine what it would be like to be at such odds with them. Nora probably wanted some space, but I wished that there were something I could do to help.

"Hey Ethan," I said, tearing his attention away from his phone. "You got any plans for the next few days?"

"Nah, why?"

"How would you feel about getting away for a couple days? I was thinking we could go somewhere fun with the girls."

"Sounds awesome, count me in. What's the plan?"

The rest of the night was spent working out the details for a little trip with the girls. We wanted to surprise them, so we made sure they were free without giving anything away. It would be nice to spend some time all together and have some fun. We all needed a break. Nora was dealing with her parents, I was stressed about my interview, and Ethan and Susie had been busy planning their wedding. Hopefully this would be exactly what we all needed.

chapter nine

Nora

I hated fighting with my parents. They had always been, and probably always would be, the only two people on the planet that I couldn't stand up to and hold my own against. When it came to anyone else, I was tough as nails and would never back down from a fight.

During my junior year of high school, I had been eating in the cafeteria one day when I saw a stuck-up senior cheerleader picking on some poor, skinny freshman with glasses. I was so infuriated that I jumped up from my table and threw myself in the middle. Even though it wasn't my fight, and she had at least six inches on me in height, I couldn't stand seeing anyone treated that way. Jake and Ethan had to pull me off her, because I'd been about three seconds away from punching that stupid bitch right in her face. I'll always remember the look on Jake's face when he pulled me away from her, like he was so proud of me even though I probably seemed like a crazy person. He loved that tough-girl side of me that wasn't afraid of a fight. Unfortunately, that tough girl ran and hid like a coward when it came to my parents. I could only imagine how disappointed Jake would be if he'd been there to witness it.

It was no secret that my parents could be controlling, and obviously what they did with Jake was way out of line. But deep down, they were still my parents, and I loved them. They had raised me and loved me my whole life, and they'd always taken care of me. I'd been fortunate enough to grow up with everything I could ever possibly want, and I was so grateful to them for providing me with that. Sure, they were controlling when it came to my future, but I knew they only wanted the best for me. Maybe this was just the price I had to pay for having such a good life. How could I stand up for myself without coming across as a spoiled, unthankful brat?

When they had returned home, I'd confronted them about what they'd done four years ago, and my dad hadn't even had the decency to act remorseful about it. He played it off as though his actions were completely justified, and that it was perfectly natural for him to interfere with my life and lie to me.

"You threatened Jake to make him stay away from me, and then let me believe that he had just abandoned me! You saw how miserable and heartbroken I was, and still you said nothing. How could you have done that to me?"

"Nora, I did what needed to be done. That boy was not, and never will be, good enough for you. He would have dragged you down with him and then eventually left you. As your father, it is my job to protect you and make sure you stay on the right path. You were ready to give up everything we'd worked so hard for... and for what? Puppy love? To be with some loser who is going nowhere fast? I'm sorry that I hurt you, but I did what was necessary to keep you from making a terrible decision, and I stand by it. Look at all you've accomplished! I only hope that you aren't making the same mistake again."

And with that he had turned and walked away, effectively ending the conversation and shutting me down. I was completely bewildered. In that moment, I realized that there was no point in arguing with him. He saw me as a child who he could control, and I let him because I could never stand up for myself. He would use any means necessary in order to get me exactly where he wanted me, and would never accept me any other way. I would forever be under his thumb.

With that realization I had gone upstairs, called Susie, and packed a bag. I needed to get away from them, at least for a little while. There were a lot of things that I needed to figure out, and I wasn't ready to do that just yet. Sure, maybe I was avoiding my issues, but if I was going to be forced to choose between my family and my future, shouldn't I know exactly what I would be giving up? I didn't know what this thing was between Jake and me. For all I knew it was just a summer fling. Either way, I had the rest of the summer ahead of me before I needed to decide anything, so I might as well take advantage of it.

Susie and I stood outside in her driveway while we waited for the boys to pick us up. They had arranged some kind of getaway for the four of us, but they were keeping the destination a surprise. Aside from the instructions they'd given us to pack enough for a couple days, we were completely in the dark. This was turning into a frequent theme with Jake, and if he kept it up, I was going to have to start planning some surprises of my own. I was anxious to see him again after our amazing night together. Just thinking about it sent shivers up my spine. I couldn't think of anything I'd rather do than spend a few uninterrupted days with him. It would definitely keep my mind off my parents.

When they pulled up in Ethan's Ford Explorer, I was even more curious about what we could possibly be doing. The back looked like it was stuffed to the brim, and they had even more stuff piled up on the roof rack.

"Howdy there, ladies!" Jake said as he hopped out of the passenger side and strolled over to us. "Who's ready to go camping?"

Susie and I exchanged looks, unsure of whether to be nervous or excited about the plan they'd devised. They were both wearing megawatt smiles, and their enthusiasm was contagious, so we gave them our bags so they could load them into the car.

"Where are we headed, boys?" Susie asked.

"Hunting Island," Ethan said, opening the passenger door and helping Susie climb in. "Think you girls can handle it, or are you afraid to go a couple days without a hair dryer?"

"Oh we can handle it," I said. "Don't you worry!" I climbed into the back seat with Jake following behind me, guiding me into the middle seat so I would be next to him. Once we were settled in, he thread his fingers through mine and rested our joined hands on his lap, caressing his thumb over mine in a way that sent heat waves flooding through my body. By the time we reached the highway, I was wishing we were alone so he could press me into the seat and put out the fire he'd started. I said a silent prayer that we wouldn't have to share a tent with Susie and Ethan during this little trip.

Hunting Island was only about twenty minutes away from Beaufort and had one of the most popular state parks and beach areas in all of South Carolina. There was a long stretch of beach, a fishing pier, wildlife center and nature trails. It was the perfect place for camping, with an area right along the beach that had restrooms, showers and even a small convenience store. At the height of the summer, it was normally packed with people, but we were going early enough in the season that we would probably have the place to ourselves. We'd talked about camping here when we were younger but had never followed through, and I was thrilled that we were finally doing it.

It was early afternoon when we pulled up to the campground, and the only other people around looked like they were packing up and getting ready to leave. It was a nice, open area that was shaded by tall palmetto trees, and a flimsy wooden fence was the only thing separating the campground from the dunes and the sandy beach. The blue water of the Atlantic Ocean stretched out as far as we could see. I couldn't wait to dip my toes in the water.

Once we found a perfect place to set up, we began unpacking all our gear. Susie and I were itching to get out on the beach to catch some afternoon sun, so the boys offered to set everything up while we walked over to the bathrooms to change into our bathing suits. I threw a cover-up on over my white bikini and waited outside for Susie. After stopping to give Jake and Ethan each a quick kiss to thank them for setting up, we grabbed towels and sunscreen, and made our way down the short path that led to the beach.

The beach extended for miles in both directions, scattered with driftwood from fallen palmetto trees that stuck out of the sand, giving it an almost eerie look. The ocean was calm and the small waves were rolling in on the shore, making the surface of the sand look glassy and smooth before retreating back. There was a gentle breeze, but with the sun high in the sky, the air was hot, making it a perfect day to be on the beach.

Leaving my towel and flip-flops in the sand, I walked down to the water's edge to put my feet in. It was cold at first; the water temperature hadn't quite caught up to the air, but it was a refreshing change from the lakes and inlets I was used to.

"Are you gonna go in?" Susie asked, coming up behind me and joining me at the water.

"Not yet. I'm going to go lay out for a bit, and maybe I'll go in once I'm nice and warm."

One we'd found a spot to settle in, we took off our cover-ups and laid our towels out on the sand.

"You know, I had my doubts about this whole 'surprise getaway' thing," Susie said, positioning herself beside me. "But I have to give props to the guys for this one, this is perfect."

"Mmm, yeah it is. Since when did those two get so smart?" I stretched out and closed my eyes, relaxing my entire body as the sun warmed my skin.

It wasn't long before our peaceful moment was interrupted by the arrival of Jake and Ethan, who had changed into their swim trunks and carried a cooler filled with beer and sandwiches. They greeted us briefly before moving a little ways down the beach to toss the football around, and I reached into the cooler to grab a couple of beers. I handed one to Susie and cracked mine open while my eyes drifted over to watch Jake. He had his shirt off and his skin was practically glistening under the hot sun. My eyes were glued to his hard abs and the toned muscles of his back and chest as he moved and stretched, reminding me of the way his muscles flexed when he was positioned above me, moving deep inside me. Heat automatically pooled to my center, and I could feel the blush rise to my cheeks. *Jeez, I've only had sex twice and I've already turned into some kind of nympho!*

"Like what you see?"

"What?" I tore my eyes away from Jake and turned to see Susie grinning at me.

"Couldn't help but notice the drool pouring from your mouth while you ogled your man's goodies," she teased. "It's just like in high school when we used to get all hot watching their football games."

I laughed because it was true. "What is it about guys playing football? I remember Jake and I going at it like crazy after one of their games. I guess some things never change."

"Speaking of going at it… it's time for you to spill, Nora! How was it? Was it worth all the hype? And don't even pretend like you two didn't do it, because I've seen the goofy smiles you two have been passing back and forth."

There was no use lying to Susie because she knew me better than anyone. I didn't even bother trying to deny it. "Definitely worth all the hype," I grinned.

"I KNEW IT!" she squealed, clapping her hands excitedly. "It's about damn time. I want details!"

Without going too deep into the specifics, I told Susie enough to satisfy her interest and get her to shut up about it before the boys came back. She still had a giddy smile on her face when they sauntered back over to us.

"Well done, Jake," Susie said, grinning up at him in a painstakingly obvious way. "With the football, I mean."

"Thanks, Sus," he said, planting a quick kiss on my cheek and winking over at Susie, completely aware of her innuendo but unfazed by it. "Who wants to go for a swim?"

"Maybe in a little while," I said, lying back down on my towel. "I'm not hot enough yet."

"Oh, you're definitely hot enough," Jake said with a devious smile. "Now get that fine ass up and come into the water with me!"

Before I had a chance to protest, he grabbed me by the waist and threw me over his shoulder, clamping his arm over my legs as he walked toward the water.

"Jake! Knock it off!" I smacked his butt playfully, trying to wriggle from his grip.

"Sorry, baby, we're goin' in."

He plunged into the ocean, tossing me into the water before diving in after me. It was a little chilly, but after spending so much time in the sun, it actually felt really good. I stood up in the chest-deep water, and a few seconds later Jake's head popped up next to me.

"Pretty nice, huh?" he said, running his hands through his wet hair.

"You're such a jerk!" I pushed his head down, dunking him underwater, and tried to swim away when he grabbed me from beneath the surface. He came back up, still holding me around the waist. I wrapped my arms and legs around him as he moved us into the deeper water. Leaning in, I placed my lips softly on his and he responded immediately, moving his lips against mine. I could taste the saltwater on his mouth as I sucked on his bottom lip, causing him to groan and deepen the kiss.

"I haven't stopped thinking about you since the other night," he grumbled against my lips. "I've been losing my mind. If I didn't get some alone time with you soon, I might have just mauled you right in front of Susie and Ethan."

He caressed his tongue against mine and I tightened my grip around him as the water sloshed around our shoulders. His hands gripped my bottom, creeping underneath my bathing suit as he pulled me firmly against him. When his hardness pressed to my center, I moaned into his mouth and rocked my hips into him, desperate to feel more.

"Ah, you're trying to drive me crazy, aren't you?" His hand slid further under my bathing suit, and he slowly pushed his finger inside me.

My hands moved to his hair, grasping it tightly as he continued to move his finger in and out of me while rubbing my sensitive flesh with his thumb. My body trembled as he took me to the edge, his mouth absorbing my cries as I went over, pulsing around him.

"Damn baby, you're so sexy," he murmured in my ear. "I love watching you come apart."

"I think it's you that's trying to drive me crazy," I said once I'd finally caught my breath.

As we pulled apart from each other, I was relieved to see that Susie and Ethan were still resting up on the beach, unaware of our little show in the water. As I climbed out I noticed that Jake had stayed in.

"Are you coming?" I asked.

"Interesting choice of words," he said, a grin tilting the corner of his mouth. "I'm just going to stay in here for a couple minutes, otherwise our friends are going to get an eyeful."

Jake

After doing a few mathematical equations in my head to calm myself down and get rid of my hard-on, I got out of the water and rejoined my friends on the beach. I expected some wise cracks from Susie and Ethan about my PDA fest with Nora, but thankfully they didn't seem to have noticed. Not that they would have been able to see anything too explicit because we were mostly underwater, but whenever I was with Nora I had a tendency to forget about anyone else but her. I would probably need to be a little more careful about groping her in public.

Grabbing a beer and a sandwich from the cooler, I sat down on my towel to eat. Nora was lying face down on her towel, giving me a front row seat to stare at her long, toned legs and perfect ass. Her little white bikini barely covered it, and her tan skin was still wet from the ocean and glistened in the sun. I had to look away before I got too excited and had to go back in the ocean and cool myself off. Again. She had me so worked up while we were in the water that it was a miracle that my cock wasn't still at full attention. I loved the way she looked and felt when she was coming apart in my arms, and I loved being the one to make her feel that good. I couldn't wait until tonight when I could bury myself deep inside her. Just thinking about it had me adjusting my shorts. Again.

I still hadn't had a chance to talk to her about what was going on with her parents. I wanted to know where her head was at and make sure she was okay. She hadn't made any attempt to talk to me about it, but I hoped it was only because we hadn't had a chance to be alone yet. When Susie and Ethan headed into the ocean, I asked Nora to walk to the lighthouse with me, and she nodded eagerly.

It was quiet on the beach, and aside from a couple of families and some young kids digging in the sand, we had the place to ourselves. I reached for Nora's hand, and we walked in silence for a while, both of us quietly taking in the peaceful setting around us. Erosion had taken a huge toll on the beach in recent years, and in certain areas there was only a narrow strip of beach left between the ocean and the tree line. They called this area of the beach "The Boneyard" because the encroaching seawater left dead trees scattered in its wake, buried on the beach with their smooth, bare branches sticking out of the sand.

The lighthouse towered well above the tops of the trees, standing out against the blue backdrop of the sky. It was open to the public, and the view from the top was incredible.

"What do you think?" Nora said, turning to me. "Should we make the trek to the top?"

"I'm game if you are." I let her lead the way inside, following her up the spiral staircase to the top. After 167 steps, we finally reached the platform, and it was totally worth it.

"Wow." She walked up to the railing to take in the amazing view of the ocean and state park beneath us.

I stood next to her, resting my elbows on the railing and turned toward her. "So, I take it things didn't go well with your parents."

Her gaze remained fixated on the view, but her expression changed. "It didn't *go* at all," she said. "As usual, they just shut me down, and it was over before it even began. No remorse. No explanation. Instead they turned it around on me, treating me like I'm still some stupid kid who can't make her own decisions. And did I stick up for myself? No. I backed down like I always do and let them win." She finally turned to me, tears welling up in her beautiful green eyes. "What is wrong with me? Why am I such a coward?"

I hated seeing her so upset, and this was exactly why I hadn't wanted to tell her about her dad in the first place. Pulling her toward me, I reached up and cupped her face in my hand. "There is nothing wrong with you, Nora. You love your parents, and you want to make them happy. There is nothing cowardly about you. You're the strongest, toughest girl I've ever met, but you're also sweet and sensitive, and you don't want to hurt the ones you love. That doesn't make you a coward. And you didn't just back down this time – you left. You showed them that what they did wasn't okay, and that was a big step. I know you have it in you to stand up to them, when you're ready, if you decide to."

Nora burrowed her face into my chest, and I held her close. As much as I wanted answers about us, and our future, I knew she didn't have them yet, and I wouldn't push her for them. For now she needed time, and I would give her that. I never wanted to see her upset, and I certainly didn't want to be the one to make her feel that way. All I ever wanted to do was make her happy. There was still a chance she could end up breaking my heart in a couple months, but I would just have to have faith in her – in us.

"Maybe we forget about all this for a while. Put it on hold," I said, wiping the tears from her face. "For now, let's focus on the fun stuff instead."

"Thank you, Jake," she whispered.

Ethan and Susie were just starting to pack up when we got back to our spot on the beach.

"Perfect timing," Ethan said when he saw us. "I'm ready for a shower and some fuckin' food!"

We hauled our beach stuff back to the campsite, and then went over to the bathrooms so we could each take a shower. There was no way the girls would have agreed to go camping if there weren't hot showers available, so I was thankful that we had picked this spot. I'd been pretty tired when we left the beach, but after a shower and a change of clothes, I felt like a whole new man.

It was warm outside, and it looked like it was going to be a gorgeous night, so Ethan and I set up the grill on the beach. We had packed hot dogs and hamburgers in the cooler, with lots of ice, to cook for dinner tonight, so we started cooking as soon as the grill was ready. The girls brought paper plates and utensils while I set up our chairs around the fire, and once the food was ready, we all sat down and ate.

Dinner was simple, but delicious. It was amazing how much better something could taste when it was being eaten on the beach next to a fire, surrounded by great friends. We stayed out on the beach long after it got dark, drinking beers and talking. The moon and stars were crystal clear against the dark sky, illuminating the beach and reflecting on the water.

We all had a pretty good buzz going, so when the girls started yawning, Ethan and I sent them back to the tents while we put everything away. Our tents were adequately separated from each other to give us a little privacy. I said goodnight to Ethan and walked over to the tent I was sharing with Nora. I'd been looking forward to finally having her to myself, so I hoped that she hadn't already fallen asleep. Bending over, I unzipped the door to the tent and climbed inside.

"Took you long enough," she whispered from underneath the blankets.

"Sorry, baby, if I'd known you were waiting, I would've hurried up." I kicked off my shoes and let my eyes adjust to the darkness of the tent. "Did you miss me?"

"Mmmm hmmm…"

She kneeled up and let the blankets fall around her, revealing the oversize t-shirt she was wearing with nothing but her sexy little boy shorts underneath. My eyes landed on her chest, and I could tell she didn't have a bra on because I could make out the outline of her breasts. I saw the hard points of her nipples through the fabric, and my dick pressed against my zipper as my body instantly reacted to her. *Fuck, she's sexy.*

When I met her gaze I could see the desire in her eyes. I instantly dropped to my knees next to her, crushing my mouth against hers. I reached down, grabbing her ass in my hands and pulling her toward me as her mouth moved furiously against mine.

My hands slid up to her waist, skimming underneath her shirt as I let my hands graze the warm skin of her back. Dropping my mouth to the curve of her neck I began nuzzling and sucking her smooth skin, eliciting a soft moan from her that drove me wild.

Her hands moved between us, fumbling with the button on my jeans as I ripped my shirt over my head, flinging it to the side before reaching for her again. Once she finished undoing my jeans she pushed on my chest, guiding me to lie down on my back before tugging my jeans the rest of the way off. My cock stood proudly underneath my boxer briefs, and I could see her gaze fall to it hungrily before she climbed over me and straddled my waist.

I grabbed her by the hips and positioned her warm pussy over me, letting her feel exactly how bad I wanted her. She sat up and pulled her shirt over her head, giving me a flawless view of her round, full tits. I reached up and took one in my hand, rubbing my thumb over her taut nipple.

"I want you so bad, baby."

"Patience," she said, looking down at me wickedly. "You took such good care of me today, and now it's time for me to return the favor."

Sliding down my body, she lowered my boxers, letting my erection spring free, and crouched over me on her knees. She grabbed my dick in her hands, stroking it gently before covering it with her hot mouth. I groaned loudly as she wrapped her lips around me, sucking me hard from base to tip, and my hands slipped into her hair as her tongue caressed my silky skin.

"Ah, fuck, baby... so good... oh, yeah..." I was having a hard time forming any thoughts, and it felt so damn good I knew I wouldn't last much longer.

It wasn't the first time she'd done this – we'd done it when we were in high school – but I had forgotten how incredible she was at it. This girl knew how to turn me on like nobody else. But as amazing as it felt, I wanted to be inside her and make her feel good too, and I couldn't do that if I exploded in her mouth right now.

I hauled her up and rolled on top of her, nestling between her legs against her slick entrance. "I need to be inside you, Nora."

Reaching for my jeans, I pulled out my wallet to get a condom.

"Hurry up," she whimpered. "I need you."

My fingers dug inside for a foil packet but came up empty. "Oh, fuck."

"What's wrong?"

"I don't have any," I flung my wallet aside and hung my head in defeat. "Shit Nora, I'm so, so sorry."

"You've never done it without one?"

"No, of course not. Never."

"Well, I've obviously never done it without one either and I'm on the pill, so…"

"You are?" I was surprised.

"Yeah, I have been since high school. My mom never believed me when I told her that we weren't having sex back then. As much as she hated the thought of me having sex, the idea of me being a pregnant teen was even worse, so she put me on the pill, and I never bothered going off it."

"Are you sure?" As badly as I wanted to be with her, I didn't want to do anything that she wasn't comfortable with.

"Yes." She grabbed my hips and pulled me toward her, where she was wet and waiting for me. "Please, Jake? Don't make me beg."

There was no way in hell I was going to argue with her. I met her mouth with mine and slowly began easing inside her. She was warm and tight, and it was unlike anything I'd ever felt before.

"Holy shit, Nora ..."

"Does it feel different?" she asked, arching her body into mine.

"You have no idea." I pushed the rest of the way into her, unable to contain the sounds that escaped from my throat. "Fuck, you feel so amazing, baby. I never knew it could feel like this."

I trailed kisses down her throat and over her collarbone, caressing her breast with my hand. I was consumed with sensation as I slid in and out of her, and I had to keep my pace slow so that I wouldn't finish too quickly. She cried out in pleasure, wrapping her legs around my waist, and I felt like I was going explode any second.

Soon her hips were lifting to meet mine with each thrust, encouraging me to move faster inside her. I knew she was getting close so I let go of my restraint and began pumping into her harder and deeper, no longer able to hold back.

"Oh God, Jake," she cried out.

I could feel her tightening around me as she came apart underneath me, screaming out my name. The pleasure on her face as she rode the waves of her release sent me over the edge, and with one final thrust I lost myself inside her.

Rolling onto my side, I leaned down and planted a gentle kiss on her lips as I held her. "Damn, baby," I said, my heart hammering out of my chest. "That was… unbelievable."

She nodded, her chest still rising and falling as she tried to catch her breath. I pulled the blankets up over us and held her close as we drifted off to sleep.

chapter ten

Nora

As the sound of seagulls broke into my dreams, my eyes flickered open just as the sun was beginning to rise. Jake's hard chest was pressed up against my back, our bodies fitting together perfectly like two pieces of a puzzle. His arm was draped around my stomach, and I could feel his warm breath tickling my ear. Shifting slightly, I felt his morning wood pressed up against me and desire shot through my entire body.

Maybe it was because I'd been missing out on sex for all these years, or maybe it was the intensity of my feelings for Jake, but for whatever reason I couldn't seem to get enough of him. My body was practically humming with anticipation. He was sleeping soundly, but I knew that there was no way I would be able to wait until tonight. No way.

I pushed my bottom against him gently, hoping to stir him awake, but he didn't move. Then I did it again, this time pressing my cheeks more firmly, rubbing against the length of his hardness. He groaned into my ear, tightening the arm around my waist as his hand moved up to caress my breast. Heat pooled between my legs at his touch, and I wiggled my butt against him teasingly.

"Mmmm, good morning," he said in a low, husky voice as he ran his fingers over my hardened nipple. "I think you're teasing me, Nora Montgomery, and there are consequences for that."

He traced his hand down my stomach and along my hip, leaving a trail of heat on my skin everywhere he touched. I was so turned on I could hardly form any words.

"Wh–what consequences?" I stuttered.

His hand moved down my inner thigh, lifting it gently and resting my leg on top of his. My breaths started coming in faster, panting in anticipation of what he was going to do next, and when he stroked the tip of his shaft along my slick, wet center, I felt like I might explode if he didn't enter me soon.

"Damn ... always ready for me, Nora. I fucking love that."

In one swift motion he pushed inside me, and I cried out in pleasure. His hand grasped onto my hip as he thrust into me from behind in a slow rhythm, filling me with long, hard strokes. I could already feel my body climbing, building up to a powerful release as his tempo gradually began to increase. When he reached his hand between my legs and began caressing me with his clever fingers, I moaned loudly and came hard around him.

Jake quickened his pace, kneading my swollen breasts with his eager hands while continuing to hammer in and out of me. His swift, deep thrusts drew out my orgasm, making it seem to go on forever as the pleasure continued to pulse within me. Finally he stilled, groaning out my name as he exploded inside of me.

His body relaxed, but we remained joined together as Jake caressed my skin with his hands and his lips. I would have been content to spend the whole day doing nothing else, but when we heard Susie and Ethan's voices outside, we reluctantly we pulled apart and threw some clothes on before they barged in and caught us with our pants down. Literally.

After wolfing down a quick breakfast, we decided to go to the pier on the other side of the park to go fishing. We piled into Ethan's SUV and made the short drive to the inlet on the other side of the park.

It was crazy to me that only a month or so ago I'd been in New York City, fighting the crowd for a seat on the subway, and now I was walking down a wooden pier with a fishing pole in my hand, surrounded by nature. The closest I got to nature in New York was the occasional walk through Central Park in between classes. It was a whole other world, and in a lot of ways, I was a different person when I was there. I hadn't really minded being in the city for school; it was fast-paced and exciting, but could I really spend another three years there? I felt like I was split in half down the middle, being pulled in opposite directions. I could feel the tension beginning to consume me, so I pushed my thoughts aside and tried to focus on the here-and-now. There was plenty of time to stress out about my life later.

The long pier extended into the deep water of the inlet, and only a short distance across the way was Fripp Island. Because the inlet was fed by the Atlantic Ocean, it had a wide variety of fish coming through, making it a popular place for both locals and tourists to fish.

It was another beautiful day, and a handful of people were already scattered along the length of the pier, leaning up against the wooden railing with their poles in hand as they waited for the fish to bite. A few more serious fishermen were already packing up for the day after what was probably a very early morning.

While the boys stopped by the visitor's center to buy some bait, Susie and I carried our poles down to the end of the pier to claim a spot. She was quiet as we walked, which was unusual for her, and I wondered what might be bothering her. Before I had a chance to ask her what was going on, Jake and Ethan returned with the bait, so I made a mental note to talk to her later on.

"What are you waiting for, Nora?" Jake said, holding out the bucket of slimy shrimp to me. "Get on in there!"

I could tell by the smirk on his face that he was expecting me to squirm away in disgust, so I decided to do just the opposite.

"Don't mind if I do!" I plunged my hand into the bucket, pulling out a nice, fat shrimp, and then smoothly thread it onto my hook without hesitating. Once it was perfectly attached, I looked up at Jake and Ethan's shocked faces. "What? Never seen anyone bait a hook before?"

Jake whistled in appreciation. "Damn! Glad to see you've still got some country in you. That was fucking sexy!"

"Tail first too," Ethan said. "I'm so proud!" He gave me high-five and then turned to Susie, holding out the bucket to her. "How 'bout you, babe?"

Susie glared at him without saying a word. Ethan seemed to take the hint, reaching for her fishing pole to bait her hook for her. She was obviously upset about something, but I'd never seen her like this. The fights between her and Ethan didn't typically last very long and mostly consisted of a lot of yelling, followed by a lot of "making up" behind closed doors. The fact that she was so quiet had me worried, and I hoped that whatever was going on with them wasn't too serious.

Tension had settled in the air around us, so I tried to diffuse it so we could get back to fishing. "Shall we make things interesting?" I asked, sliding my aviators down my nose so I could look Jake in the eyes. "Whoever catches the biggest fish doesn't have to gut and prepare whatever we catch?"

Jake grinned. "Game on!"

It wasn't long before Jake had his first catch of the day, followed shortly after by Ethan. However, both fish were a little too small to keep so they were thrown back.

The hot summer sun beat down on us from above, increasing the temperature as the day went on, and I was glad to be dressed in just jean shorts and a tank top. I was even more thankful that Jake had lent me one of his old, beat up baseball hats to wear. It was worn in and faded, but I could remember the exact day he bought it and put it on for the first time. It had been a deep, navy blue then, and I'd loved the way it brought out the dark blue flecks in Jake's eyes. He was wearing a different baseball hat now, and I found myself thinking about when he'd gotten it and wondering if some other girl had helped him pick it out.

The idea of that immediately sent a pang of jealousy running through me, which was stupid, but I couldn't help it. If I could feel so resentful about a fictitious girl, I didn't even want to imagine how I would feel about someone real. Obviously I couldn't change the past, but I hated that Jake and I had lost such a big chunk of time that we could have been together.

And yet you're still thinking about leaving again.

My subconscious thoughts were interrupted when Jake started reeling something in. The muscles in his arm strained against his white t-shirt as he pulled against whatever he'd caught, and I was so distracted by him that I almost didn't notice when something started tugging on my own line.

"Got something, Nora?" Ethan asked.

Holding tightly onto my fishing rod, I braced myself and started spinning the reel to bring it in. Whatever I had on the end of my line was pretty big, and it wasn't long before my forehead was beading with sweat, my hands were slipping, and I was losing the battle to the fish. Just when I thought I was beat, I felt Jake come up and stand behind me.

"Hang in there babe, you got it," he said, reaching his arms around me to grab hold of my pole. "You reel, I'll pull. Ready?"

We worked together to haul in what turned out to be a big trout; even bigger than the drum fish Jake had caught. Both were keepers, so we put them on ice in the cooler to keep them fresh while we continued fishing.

As the day wore on we all caught more fish, but aside from a good-sized trout that Susie caught, they were all thrown back. My fish was still the biggest of the day, and Ethan was the only one who hadn't caught anything worth keeping.

"I didn't want to make you guys look bad!" Ethan joked. "So I let you guys win. You're welcome!"

"Sure ya did E," Jake laughed. "Don't be embarrassed that your girl has more skills than you."

I put the last of my fishing gear in the tackle box and closed the lid. "Well, it sounds like you two have everything under control here," I said, grabbing Susie's arm as we started walking down the pier. "So, we're just going to go have some girl time while you guys do all the gutting and cleaning, mmm'kay?"

"Sounds good to me!" Susie called out over her shoulder as we walked away from them.

"Of course it does!" Ethan yelled to us. "You chicks always stick together!"

We laughed and kept walking down the dock. The boys wouldn't have trusted us to prepare the fish anyway, so we didn't feel bad about leaving them to do the dirty work. Besides, they were boys – they loved all that gross crap.

After grabbing cold drinks and snacks from the visitor's center, and dropping some of it off to the boys, we walked across the highway to the marsh boardwalk. The wooden boardwalk extended over the tidal marsh and creek, leading us to a covered platform area where we could sit and enjoy the peaceful scenery around us. For a while we sat in silence, just watching the birds while we ate, both famished from a long day of fishing in the sun.

"So," Susie said, breaking the silence. "This thing with you and Jake, is it for real?"

Normally I loved the fact that Susie cut through the bullshit and got right to the chase, but she had asked me the one question

I'd been trying to avoid.

"I don't know," I answered honestly. "I mean, I think it is, but we haven't really talked about it."

"Why not?"

"Because, there's still a lot of stuff to figure out, and it's too soon to get into all that right now."

"What you really mean is that *you* haven't talked about it, because you're avoiding it, and Jake is too scared to bring it up himself."

Damn. She was good, I had to give her that. I should have known she would have me all figured out.

"Nora," she said, turning to face me. "Do you want to be with him or not?"

"Maybe, but how can I know for sure? I've never even been with anyone else."

"Yeah, because you've been hung up on Jake ever since you met, and no one else ever got to you. Doesn't that tell you something?"

She was right, of course. I'd been on a few dates, but I'd never felt even a fraction of what I feel for Jake. Not to mention that the thought of him with anyone else gave me instant nausea.

"Alright, Sus. I get your point. I know I have some decisions to make, and I promise I'll work it out soon, okay?

"Fine," she smiled. "I know I'm a nag, but it's only because I don't want to see you two all sulky and depressed and heartbroken again. It was a drag!"

"Fair enough!" I laughed, glad to be out of the hot seat. "Now it's your turn. What the *hell* is going on with you and Ethan?"

"It's all this wedding stuff," she sighed. "We've been bickering so much about everything. Ethan is getting so fed up with it all that now he says he wishes we could just elope. Here I am trying to make sure everything is perfect, and it's like he doesn't care about our wedding at all."

I tried not to laugh, but I was so relieved that there was nothing major going on with them that I couldn't help it. I should have known they would be fine. I'd never known two people more perfect for each other than those two idiots.

"It's not funny!" she glared at me.

"I'm sorry," I told her. "But Susie, Ethan is a *guy*. Of course he's not enthused about planning a wedding. If your biggest problem is that he's so anxious to marry you that he wants to elope, then I think you two are in pretty good shape."

"You think so?"

"I know so."

Jake

The next morning we packed up the campsite, loaded everything into the SUV and started the short trip home. As much as we all would have liked to stay there in our little paradise, it was time to get back to reality.

I sat in the back with Nora while Susie and Ethan basically groped each other in the front seats. They had resolved whatever was going on between them, and now they were on to the next phase: make-up sex.

"I don't know what's worse," Nora whispered in my ear. "Dealing with my parents or having to share a wall with those two and listen to their sexcapades!"

"If those were my options, I think I'd choose to sleep on the lawn," I told her, and she giggled. "So I guess it's a good thing you're coming home with me."

"What?" She turned to me with a puzzled expression. "You don't have to do that, I don't want to intrude."

"Nora, don't be crazy. You're my girl, and you're going to

stay with me for as long as you want until you sort things out with your folks. Okay?"

"Are you sure?"

"Of course I'm sure," I smiled. "You are staying with me, end of story." Ethan pulled up to my house and parked alongside the curb. "Now get your stuff and come with me before these two start doing it right in front of us."

I unloaded all our stuff from the car and threw it on the porch to deal with it later. We barely managed to say goodbye to Susie and Ethan before they screeched out and started hightailing it down the road to their place. I started walking inside but stopped when I saw the look of apprehension on Nora's face.

"Come on, babe," I said, grabbing her hand and leading her up the front steps.

"I can't believe I haven't seen your place yet," she commented, following eagerly behind me.

I swung open the front door and led her inside. "Well, there's not much to it, but make yourself at home. Mi casa es su casa, baby."

She glanced around curiously, still holding her bag. "Is the whole house yours?"

"No, it's split up into two apartments, and I just rent the first floor." I grabbed her bag and plopped it down on the floor next to mine. "The owner of the house is an older couple, and they use the second floor whenever they're in town. They spend most of their time in Florida, though, so they're rarely here. They give me a good deal on rent in exchange for maintaining the place and keeping an eye on things for them."

"Aren't you going to give me the grand tour?" she asked, her eyes sparkling with curiosity.

"Right this way, beautiful."

I led her through the small entryway and into the living area. There was a slightly faded brown leather couch with a matching recliner, a coffee table, and an old television that my parents had passed down to me when they'd gotten a new one. The wood floor was fairly scuffed up, and there was a green area rug that, like most of the furniture, was here when I moved in. Max's dog bed sat in the corner along with some of his old, chewed up toys. My parents had taken him while we went camping, and I had almost forgotten that I needed to pick him up.

"It's so... neat," she said as we moved through the room. "I'm impressed."

"You caught me on a good day," I smiled, bringing her into the next room. "Here we have the kitchen, where I whip up all my exquisite cuisine. You'll get to experience that soon enough."

When I'd first moved in, the kitchen was a wreck, but after painting the cabinets a glossy white and re-grouting the tile floor, it actually didn't look half bad. There was a small table with a few chairs tucked in the corner, which I'd probably used a grand total of two times since I'd been here. Since I was almost always alone, I normally ate in the living room in front of the television, or on one of the stools at the breakfast bar.

I took Nora through the French doors off the kitchen that led outside to a nice back porch and a small grassy yard. It wasn't much, but it was great for grilling and was totally fenced-in so Max could hang outside and I never had to worry about him running off.

We walked back inside, and Nora looked up at me expectantly.

"I think you're forgetting an important part of the tour," she said, a playful gleam in her eyes as she gestured toward my bedroom door.

She was so damn adorable.

"Ladies first." I opened the door to my bedroom, gesturing her through, and then followed in behind her.

I didn't spend much time in here, other than while I was sleeping, so I'd never done much with the space. All I needed were the basic necessities, most of which had already been here when I moved in. There was a full-size bed centered on the back wall, neatly made with my navy blue comforter and matching pillows. Two small night tables sat on either side of the bed, but I only bothered to keep a lamp on the side that I used. A tall dresser was pushed up against another wall next to the small closet, and Max's dog bed was in the corner. The floors were the same worn hardwood as the living room, and the walls were just plain white because I never bothered to hang anything up. My favorite part of the room was the sliding glass doors leading to the backyard. At night I could see the moon and the stars, and in the morning the sun was usually a pretty reliable alarm clock.

Nora turned to me with a half-smile when she finished looking around. "So, this is where the magic happens?"

"Nope, no magic yet… but now that you're here we can change that," I winked.

"Oh, come on!" she said, looking at me with disbelief. "You're trying to tell me that you've never had any girls here?"

"Never," I told her honestly. "You're the first and only girl that I've wanted to have here." I reached for her hips, gently pulling her against me. "But for right now we need to get out of this room because all I can think about is ripping your clothes off and throwing you on my bed, and unfortunately I have to go to work."

Her face fell. "You have to go?"

"Only for an hour or two. I have to stop by a job site to check in and make sure everything is on schedule. Will you be okay here by yourself?"

"Yeah, I guess, but I'd rather you stay here with me." She pressed herself against me and wrapped her arms around my neck.

"Aww, baby," I groaned. "I would stay here if I could, trust me, but I promise I'll be back soon. Then nothing will stop me from having my way with you on that bed."

"Sounds like a plan," she smiled, unwrapping her arms from around my neck. "Now, get out of here and hurry back."

"Feel free to snoop around. I've got nothing to hide." I

grabbed my work boots from the closet and sat down to put them on. "Oh, except that box of porn under the bed," I joked. "But I'm just holding onto that for a friend, I swear."

She laughed, pushing me out of the room and toward the front door. "Go!"

"Seriously, though." I paused in the entryway. "Make yourself at home, okay babe?" I gave her a quick kiss and then ran out the door.

My dad's company had started a new job just outside of town and I felt a little guilty that I hadn't been to the site yet. We were only in the framing phase, so I knew they were doing just fine without me, but I still needed to put in some face time with the crew. My dad had been there while I was away and had apparently told the guys about my little romantic getaway, so the banter and ridicule began as soon as I set foot on the job site.

"Where's your *girlfriend,* Harris?" they teased. "Did she already kick you to the curb?"

"You're moving a little slow. Must be that ball and chain you're draggin' around!"

I let them have their fun and didn't let it bother me. It's just what guys do. Besides, they'd never had the chance to tease me about a girl before, so I figured I was due. It didn't help that when my phone rang, I immediately walked away to answer it because I hoped it was Nora. I never used to answer my phone while I was working.

"Somebody's whipped!" they yelled to me as I walked away.

As it turned out, it wasn't even Nora. It was an out-of-state number that I didn't recognize, so I let it go to voicemail.

Once I was finished at the site, I made a quick stop at the gro-

cery store to pick up some food. The contents in my fridge consisted of beer, hot dogs and butter. Not exactly the ingredients for a
nice dinner with your girl. The old Jake who Nora remembered
could hardly boil water, so I was eager to show her my skills and
give her a little reminder of how much I'd changed. I bought all the
fixings to make beef tenderloin and grabbed a nice bottle of wine.
The new Jake was worthy of a girl like Nora, and I intended to
show her that.

After picking Max up at my parents' house, and promising
them that I would bring Nora over to see them soon, I finally made
it home. Nora's little silver Toyota was parked out front, so Susie
must have stopped by to drop it off.

"Honey, I'm home!" I called out as I walked through the door,
my arms full of grocery bags.

Nora was on the couch in the living room, folding laundry.
She was surrounded by piles of perfectly-folded clothes and I
could hear the sound of the dryer in the background. My heart
pulled in my chest at the sight of her sitting there, perfectly comfortable doing our laundry like it was part of her everyday routine.
It felt so natural coming home and having her in my house. I didn't
want her to ever leave.

"It's about time!" she teased, looking up from the shirt she
was folding. "I hope you don't mind that I did some laundry. All
the clothes in my bag were dirty, and then I figured I'd wash the
clothes from your bag, too. And then I saw the laundry basket in
your room..."

"Baby, of course I don't mind. You're doing me a favor.
Heck, you're even folding it for me. I usually just dump it in the
drawers when it comes out of the dryer, so this is a serious up-
grade." I went into the kitchen and put the grocery bags on the
counter. "I'll have to repay you with an awesome dinner. I hope
you're hungry."

Max came bounding in from outside and immediately went
over to Nora, his tail whipping furiously back and forth in excite-

ment.

"Hey, Max! How ya doin, buddy?" she said, scratching him behind the ears and rubbing his stomach.

"Oh great," I said. "I've already been replaced by another dude!"

Nora just laughed and continued to pet him. I put the groceries away and started getting together everything I needed to make dinner.

When our meal was almost ready, I set the breakfast bar with plates, silverware and two glasses of wine. *Not bad,* I said to myself when I stepped back to look at it. Sure, the forks didn't match and the wine glasses looked more like water glasses, but still, it looked pretty damn good for my first "real" dinner.

"Okay, we're ready," I called out to Nora, who was lounging on the couch with Max at her side. "Time to put my skills to the test."

I served her first and sat there awkwardly while I watched her take a bite, nervous about whether or not she would like it.

"Wow, Jake," she said once she had swallowed it. "You are just full of surprises, aren't you? I'm officially impressed. This is delicious!"

With a sigh of relief, I finally turned to my own plate and started eating. "I aim to please, baby!"

After we had stuffed ourselves with dinner, Nora helped me clean up the kitchen and wash the dishes. We worked together in happy silence, and I was once again struck by how easy and natural it was to have her here. Everything was better when she was around, and there was no way I would ever be able to let her go. I only hoped that she felt the same way.

"What's on your agenda for tomorrow?" I asked her.

"Well, since you have to work, I'll probably head down to my dad's office. I haven't put in very much time over there, and apparently they're working on a big case right now and need a few extra hands. Fortunately my dad's in court so I won't have to see him."

I could see the flash of sadness across her face when she mentioned her dad, and I wanted to keep her mind off all that. "I have to spend the whole day away from you?" I groaned melodramatically. "I don't think I can handle it."

She moved closer to me and draped her arms around my neck, looking up at me with a teasing smile. "Is Jake Harris turning into the clingy boyfriend type?"

"Only with you, Nora," I replied softly. My heart was soaring out of my chest at her use of the word "boyfriend." At this point, it was fairly obvious that's what we were, but we'd never officially discussed it, so hearing her say it had me grinning like an idiot.

"Works for me," she said, tightening her arms around my neck and drawing her body closer to mine. "You can cling to me all you want."

All other thoughts got pushed aside when she was pressed up against me like that, and all I could think about was how badly I wanted her. Grabbing her by the hips, I lifted her up and started carrying her out of the kitchen. "Well then, I better get you in my bed so I can cling to you all night."

I brought her into my bedroom, kicking the door closed behind me, and did just that.

chapter eleven

Nora

Over the next week, Jake and I settled into our own little routine. He had to work every day, and I was busy helping out at my dad's firm, so we were up early. Our schedules meshed together perfectly. Because he often got dirty on the jobsite, Jake preferred taking his showers at night, so while I took a shower in the morning, he would make us coffee. We would eat a quick breakfast together before making our way out the door and then, after a kiss goodbye, we went our separate ways.

In the evening, when we got home we would take Max for a long walk to a nearby field in the woods at the end of the street where we could throw the ball for him. We both helped out making dinner, except for one night when we were both too tired to cook so we picked up take-out. Then, we spent the rest of the night cuddled together on the couch to watch a movie together, or I would read a book while Jake played video games. As ordinary as it seemed, there was nothing boring about it. When I was with Jake, I felt more alive than I ever had, and I was completely at peace. It was as though I was exactly where I was meant to be, making it easy to push aside all the issues that we had yet to work out.

Any idea I ever had about simply needing to get Jake out of my system before moving on had officially been put to rest. Clearly, it wasn't going to be that simple. I still got butterflies in my stomach when I left work and knew I would see him soon, and no matter how exhausted we both were at the end of the day, we still buried ourselves in each other every night.

We were drawn intensely to one another, as though we were trying to make up for all the time we'd lost. When we made love, it was sensual and unhurried as we enjoyed each other and worshipped each other's bodies. It was sexy as hell. Every touch set me on fire and left me craving more.

Of course, there were still times when it was urgent and heated. Like last night after dinner when we didn't even waste time disrobing. Instead, Jake had just hiked up my skirt, hoisted me onto the counter, slid off my panties and unzipped his pants before taking me right there in the kitchen. Just thinking about it had me practically trembling in anticipation for later that night...

"Hey, Nora, are you finished with that deposition?"

A voice broke through my daydream, and I turned to see Kathy, one of the senior associates. I scrambled to find the file among all the others that were scattered on my desk and handed it to her. "Yes, it's right here."

"Perfect," she said, glancing at it quickly before tucking it into a folder. "You're the best, Nora. I really can't thank you enough for all your help this week. I don't know how we would have done it without you."

"It's no problem," I said. "I'm happy to help, and I've enjoyed being here." Surprisingly, it was the truth. It had been much different than what I'd been expecting. Everyone at the office was really friendly, and the case we were working on was actually somewhat interesting. Of course, one week as a lawyer was a whole lot different than a lifetime, but at least it had me feeling a little better about my inevitable future.

"We hope to have you back in here soon," she said. "But in the meantime, have a great time at your friend's wedding. When do you leave?"

"The wedding isn't until next weekend, but we're heading to Charleston on Wednesday for a little girl time beforehand." In other words, the bridesmaids and I were at Susie's beck and call to help out with the last minute details and make sure Susie didn't go completely insane.

"Well, enjoy yourself. You've earned it!" Kathy smiled before heading back into her office.

I glanced up and saw my dad on the other side of the office. After quickly collecting the last of my things from the desk, I slipped out of the office before he had a chance to come over to me. Thanks to his busy court schedule, I'd managed to avoid any run-ins with him all week, and I wasn't about to have one now.

"Did you talk to your dad at all this week?"

Jake and I were out for a walk with Max, and he had finally decided to bring up the issue that we'd both been avoiding during this whole week of playing house. It had been nice to live in our own little bubble for a while, and as much as I'd like to continue on like that, I knew that we couldn't avoid our issues forever.

"Finally time to face the elephant in the room, eh?" I said.

"I think so."

We stopped walking and sat down on a bench at the entrance to the park where Max was chasing after the stick Jake had thrown for him.

"I only saw my dad a few times this week when I was at the office, and we mostly just avoided each other. I think he's trying to give me some space while I sort everything out. I've never stayed mad at him before, so he's probably just waiting for it to blow over." More like he was waiting for me to calm down and sweep it under the rug, and then do exactly what he wanted me to do like always.

"Does he know about me?"

"Probably. He hasn't said anything, but he has a way of finding that stuff out."

Jake turned to me, resting his arm along the seat behind me. "I'm just going to say one thing and then I promise to leave it alone, okay?"

I nodded, encouraging him to continue.

"You can't avoid your parents forever. Sooner or later, you gotta have it out with them and you'll be happier once you do. It doesn't have to be today, or tomorrow, or even next week, but eventually it's going to have to happen. And when it does, it will be for you. Not for me, or them, or anyone else. Just you."

"I know," I sighed. He was right. As much as I wanted to avoid confrontation with my parents, I had to face them eventually. Fall would arrive before we knew it, and then it would be too late. What Jake didn't realize was that I still didn't know *what* the hell I wanted, and I couldn't confront my parents until I figured it out.

That was the hardest part… and the part that could leave us either deliriously happy, or completely shattered.

I jolted awake at the sound of a dog barking outside. It was still dark, and moonlight was pouring in through the sliding glass doors of Jake's bedroom. Leaning up in my sleepy haze, I turned around to look at the digital clock on Jake's nightstand and saw that it was 2:38AM.

After our walk, we had put the heavy conversation behind us and enjoyed our first night together without having to worry about either of us getting up for work in the morning. We ordered a pizza and got tipsy off a couple bottles of wine, which probably explained why I was awake in the middle of the night. Whenever I drank too much wine, I had a hard time sleeping.

Jake's arms automatically tightened around me when I shifted, pulling me closer to him. I cuddled against his warm, bare chest and listened to the steady beat of his heart. Running my hand over his rippled stomach, along his heated skin and around to his back, I felt his hard, lean muscles underneath my touch, and desire stirred within me. He'd been inside of me only a few short hours ago, but I already wanted more.

I pressed my lips to his chest, brushing a trail of soft kisses up his torso to his neck and along his jaw. When I reached his ear and gently sucked his earlobe–his secret spot–he groaned, rolling over on top of me.

"Damn, woman, you're trying to kill me, aren't you?"

I giggled and wrapped my legs around him, desire stirring inside me as I felt him grow hard against me. "I can't sleep. I want you."

"God, you're so fuckin' sexy."

He crushed his mouth on mine, holding himself above me as he gently nipped and sucked my eager lips. I cried out as the ache between my legs intensified and warmth pooled in my stomach. Just when I thought he was about to sink inside me, he rolled over and pulled me on top so I was straddling him. I sat up and rocked against his hard shaft, causing him to moan loudly as he gripped my hips and guided himself inside me.

"Oh God, Jake…" I gasped as he filled me. He was so deep that I could feel every perfect inch of him. I began to move, tentatively at first, as I found my rhythm and relished being in control. I could already feel myself beginning to unravel as I started going faster, bracing my hands on his hard chest as I continued to ride him.

"Ah, fuck, you feel amazing. Just like that, baby."

Jake's words were my undoing, and I screamed out his name as I shattered around him. This time was different, though. Despite the waves pulsing through my body, it wasn't enough. My body was still keyed up and coiling with desire. I needed more.

As if he could sense it, Jake sat up and wrapped my legs around his back, pulling me against him and somehow driving even deeper inside me. Gripping my hips tightly, he thrust into me and took my breast into his mouth when I arched forward. The combination of his tongue on my nipple and his movement deep within me sent me into sensory overload. I'd never felt anything so good. All I could focus on was the pleasure rippling through me, and I had no control over the moans and cries that were slipping out of my throat.

A sheer layer of sweat covered us both as we clasped each other, driving our bodies together as we worked toward our release. I could feel it building, far more intensely than before, and when Jake plunged deep inside and then stilled, I shattered around him in a mind-blowing orgasm, clenching him tight and sending him over the edge as we cried out each other's names.

Our grip on each other loosened, but neither of us moved as we held each other and enjoyed the aftershocks. Jake rubbed my back, placing gentle kisses on my lips and along my jaw as we waited for our breathing to return to normal.

"Damn," he whispered against my ear. "Feel free to wake me up like that anytime."

The next day Jake and I were in the backyard giving Max a bath with the hose, when his phone started ringing from inside the kitchen. We were both soaking wet and soapy, but I knew that Jake was awaiting a call about the job in Charleston, so I offered to grab it while he was busy wrangling a soap-covered Max.

By the time I reached the phone it had already gone to

voicemail, but the name on the screen read "Stanley Norton." I stared at it for a few seconds, trying to figure out how I knew that name, before going back outside and handing the phone to Jake. He looked a little nervous while he listened to the voicemail, and I didn't interrupt despite the fact that my head was full of questions.

"What was that about?" I finally asked.

"A job. He actually offered me a job."

"Wait, Stanley Norton offered you a job?" It finally hit me and I remembered how I knew that name. "But doesn't he work in Louisiana?"

"Yeah, he does," Jake answered quietly.

My stomach was in knots, and all of a sudden I was angry. "So, all this time that you've been telling me how much you want to be with me and lecturing me about figuring out what I want, you were planning to move away and not tell me? What exactly would that mean for us?"

"I never said I was going to take the job, I just–"

"You just what?" I snapped, cutting him off. "You just wanted to wait and see if I would give up everything to be with you, and *then* you would leave?"

"No, of course not." His normally bright eyes were dark, but he kept his voice steady. "They sought me out to offer me an interview, and I was desperate enough to take it. It was just an interview!" He moved toward me and ran a gentle finger down my cheek. "I want to be with you. Don't you understand that? But I'm waiting around here like an idiot while you decide what the hell you want, when for all I know, you're going to take off and leave my heart in a million pieces! You wanna know what I want? I. Want. You. What the hell do you want?"

Confusion suddenly swept across his face, and he took a step back. "Wait, how did you know that he works in Louisiana?"

All of the pieces began falling into place, and I felt sick to my stomach when I realized what happened. "I know him. Stanley Norton. He–he's a friend of my father's."

Understanding washed over Jake's face, and I could tell that he had put it together. "Of course he is. FUCK!" He yelled, throwing his phone into a tree and smashing it into pieces.

I took a step backwards, unsure how to respond. I'd never seen Jake this upset before.

"Here I thought that this big firm actually sought me out because they liked my work. But no, once again it's just your dad manipulating everything to keep me away from you. God, I'm such an IDIOT! Of course they aren't interested in *me*. It doesn't matter that I worked my ass off for four years, I'm still just a fucking loser and a screw-up who can't do anything right. That's all I'll ever be!"

My heart broke inside my chest and I hated that he saw himself like that. And it was my Dad's fault. "Jake…" I attempted to reach out and comfort him.

"I have to go." He marched around the side of the house with Max following behind him, and I could hear the sound of his truck starting up and tearing out of the driveway.

I slumped to the ground and waited for the tears to come, but they didn't. Instead, anger was boiling up inside me in a way I'd never felt before. I waited for my breathing to return to normal, but it didn't. This wasn't something that could be cured with a few breathing exercises and relaxation techniques.

At twenty-two years old, my choices were still not my own. My life was not my own. It was all a big jumble of lies and manipulation disguised as good intentions. I was just a puppet in my dad's show, while he was behind the scenes pulling my strings and making me perform the scenes that he'd chosen. And I'd let him.

Not anymore.

Jake

The heartbroken look on Nora's face when I stormed off was almost enough to stop me in my tracks and keep me from leaving.

Almost. But not quite.

With all the anger that was bursting inside of me, I knew that if I stayed it would only make things worse. I had so many emotions running through me after that onslaught of information, and all I wanted to do was lash out at her, even though I knew it wasn't her fault.

As a teenager, I'd been pretty worthless. I'd accepted that. But I thought that maybe, just *maybe* I'd outgrown that part of my life and people would finally start seeing me differently. Clearly, I was wrong. I would forever be viewed as the teenage version of myself.

After driving around for a while, I found myself at the USC-Beaufort campus, where I'd struggled through four years of night classes and summer sessions to get my degree in architecture. I thought that I'd finally made something of myself and could be someone that a girl like Nora would be proud to be with. Someone that Nora's father would deem as worthy.

Nope.

To him, I would always be a fuck up. I would always be the guy that she was slumming it with until she met Mr. Perfect.

As I walked around the campus, I looked at the empty dorms and classroom buildings, trying to picture what it would have been like to experience college life the way that most students did – the freedom of living in the dorms, taking two classes a day, partying on the weekends, and then going home during the summer and getting a break from it all. I never had that.

My so-called college life had consisted of working construction full-time during the day while attending classes at night. During the summer "break" I took advantage of summer classes to make up for the credits I was missing due to the fact that I could only take classes at night.

It was easy to be envious of all my friends who had gone off and had these amazing college experiences while enjoying the freedom of living away from home. But I never resented it. I never resented the fact that I'd had to work so hard to get to where I was. I never resented having to do it all on my own because my parents couldn't afford to help me. I never resented my friends for getting to live the easy life while I was here working my ass off. I never resented all the partying and fun I had to give up in order to get enough credits to graduate. I never resented any of it.

I was grateful.

College was never a part of my plan. Okay, I could admit that when I was in high school, I'd never had anything close to a plan. But still, higher education was never on my radar, and I certainly never expected to earn a degree. When I was in high school all I did was slack off, chase girls and get into trouble, so I was extremely grateful for the fact that I was even able to attend college courses because I probably didn't deserve to be there. It didn't matter to me that I wasn't able to do it the conventional way, because at least I'd gotten a chance.

Still, I had worked my ass off to get to where I was, and I hated that Nora's father could so easily undermine everything I'd done. Would I ever be good enough for him? Or would I constantly be fighting to earn his respect?

When I was done wandering around the campus I drove straight to my parents' house. If there was anyone in the world I could trust to give me sound advice, it was them.

I sat down and told them the whole story, including the truth about what had happened when Nora first went off to college and the role her father had played in splitting us up, as well as everything that had led up to today's events and his most recent manipulations. Surprisingly, they weren't nearly as shocked about my revelations as I thought they would be.

"Honey, we always suspected he had something to do with the two of you splitting up the way you did," my mom explained, a sad look dancing across her features. "We saw the way you two were with each other, and there was no way you would break up just because of the distance or some stupid fight."

"Nora's father is a powerful man," my dad added. "He's used to getting what he wants, and he wants a certain life for his daughter. Somehow he sees you as a threat to that. There's no doubt that what he did was wrong, but in his own twisted way he thinks he's doing what's best for Nora."

"So, what do I do now?" I asked.

My dad was quiet for a couple seconds before turning to face me head on. "Well, son, you're not the same stupid kid that you were the first time around. You've worked hard and done right for yourself, and maybe it's time that he knows that. Maybe you need to show him that he can't push you around anymore."

"And when it comes to Nora, you just need to be patient," my mom said. "There's no doubt that the girl loves you, that's not what this is about. She's just so busy getting pulled in different directions trying to please everyone that she hasn't stopped to think about what she really wants. Just give her some time. She has a lot of things to sort out and it's not something you can help her with. She has to do it on her own."

She reached for my hand, giving it a quick squeeze before continuing. "If you love her as much as I think you do, then you need to let her figure out what *she* wants, and then stand by her no matter what she decides. Just be there for her. That poor girl is so afraid of losing the people she loves, that she hasn't fought for what she wants. You need to show her that you'll be there for her no matter what. Do you think you can do that?"

"Yeah, I can do that." My eyes remained glued to the floor as guilt consumed me. I'd never given much thought to everything that Nora was going through, and I felt terrible for pushing her to make decisions and confront her parents like it was an easy thing to do.

Stupid ass.

"Hey, Jake?" My father called to me while I was on my way out the door. "We couldn't be more proud of you, you know. You're a good man. Don't forget that."

"Thanks, Pops," I nodded. Closing the front door behind me, I walked outside and hopped into my truck, preparing myself to finally do something I should have done four years ago.

Once I got on the main road, I reached into my pocket for my cell phone, only to remember that I had smashed it against a tree and it was lying in pieces in my yard. Groaning, I looked around and pulled into the nearest gas station that I saw had a pay phone.

I reached into my glove box and grabbed a handful of coins from the stash I kept there before making my way to the side of the building where the pay phone was located. By some miracle it appeared to be operational, so I shoved some quarters in the slot and dialed information. After requesting the number for Norton Architectural Partners, I stayed on the line while the operator put me through, and then waited while it rang and eventually went to voicemail. I left a brief message before getting back in my truck and continuing on to my next stop.

My plan was to go straight to Nora's parents' house, but when I drove past her dad's law firm and saw his silver Mercedes sedan in the parking lot, I slowed down and found a parking spot down the street. I took a deep breath before getting out and did my best to hype myself up during the short walk down the street to the entrance of his building.

The front door was unlocked, so I pushed it open and made my way into the empty office. Given that it was the weekend, it was no surprise that it was so quiet, but I could see a couple of lights on in the offices down the hall.

As I got closer I could hear an angry voice talking on the phone and immediately recognized it as Nora's father. The door to his office was open, and I watched him slam down the phone, unaware of me standing in the doorway. I knocked gently to let him know I was there, and his head snapped up immediately.

"What the hell are you doing here?" he barked, penetrating me with an icy stare.

The murderous expression on his face was almost enough to send me running in the other direction, but I sucked it up and kept going. I had to do this. I wouldn't let him intimidate me this time. I moved toward his desk where he was now standing. "I just need a few minutes of your time, Mr. Montgomery. It will only take a moment."

"Fine. Have a seat," he grumbled, sitting back down in his expensively upholstered leather chair behind his perfectly polished mahogany desk.

I sat down in one of the chairs facing his desk and cleared my throat. In all my haste to confront him, I hadn't given much thought to what I was actually going to say.

"So what is it, Jake? You need a lawyer or something? Because I'm pretty sure I'm out of your price range."

His rude comments didn't surprise me, so I ignored them and looked him directly in the eye. "I came here to inform you that I turned it down."

"Huh?"

"The job offer that you conveniently arranged for me. I wanted you to know that I turned it down, and will do the same with any other 'offers' that you may have for me in the future."

"That seems like a pretty stupid decision, boy. I would think someone in your position ought to take what he can get."

"I appreciate the opportunity, sir. Really, I do. I know I'd be damn lucky to have a chance like that. It's a dream come true. But even though I'd love that job, I love Nora more. I'm not a scared, stupid kid anymore, and I'm not going to let you push me around this time. I intend to stick by Nora no matter what. Whether she's here, in New York, or in Timbuktu. I love her. She's the most important thing in the world to me, and I'm not going anywhere until she kicks me to the curb herself."

Nora's father was doing his best to hide his shock, and frankly, so was I. I'd never stood up to him before, and in the entire time I'd known him, I'd barely said two words to the man. I decided to take advantage of his stunned silence and keep going before he had a chance to interrupt me.

"I know you love her too, and I know you think that you're doing what's best for her. But with all due respect, sir, no one will ever love her as much as I do. I know she deserves better than me, but I will spend my whole life working to be worthy of her and making sure she has everything she could ever want. I will take care of her. Always."

I stood from the chair and started walking towards the door before turning toward him one last time. "She deserves to make her own choices, and she shouldn't have to choose between us."

With that I opened the door and left without another word.

I'd finally done it. It was about four years too late, but I'd done it. Now all I could do was hope that I hadn't completely destroyed things with Nora.

chapter twelve

Nora

The driveway in front of my parent's house was empty when I pulled up, indicating that neither my mother or father were there. I knew they wouldn't be out for too long, and this time I wasn't going anywhere until I got answers. So, instead of running off, I plopped myself down on a stool in the kitchen and waited for them to come back.

The more I thought about what had happened, the angrier I got. By the time I heard the sound of a car pulling into the driveway, anger was pulsing through me in waves, and I felt like I might explode.

"Nora! Honey, are you here?" My mother called from the doorway. "I saw your car out front."

I ignored her, not saying a single word until she made her way into the kitchen and saw me.

"Oh, there you are. I'm so glad you're here!" Oblivious to my anger, she moved toward me to give me a hug, and I recoiled from her touch.

"Did you know about it?" I asked, my expression hard and unwavering.

She looked at me blankly. "Know about what?"

"The job." I stood up so we were eye-to eye. "The job that dad arranged for Jake to get him away from me. Did you know about it?"

"Oh, Nora." The look on her face answered the question for me.

"How could you? How could you just stand there and let him control every aspect of my life without doing anything about it?" By now I was practically screaming, and my eyes were full of unshed tears. "You saw what his manipulations did to me. I spent the last four years of my life hurt, confused and looking for answers that you had all along! Dad has already cost me four years of happiness. How could you just stand there let him do it all over again?"

I looked at my mother, tears pouring down my cheeks, and for the first time, I actually saw guilt. Her shoulders were hunched in defeat, and there was sorrow in her deep green eyes.

"You're right." She met my gaze, her voice laced with regret. "I'm so sorry, Nora."

Her outright admission came as a shock to me, and as much as I wanted to stay angry at her, I was quickly running out of steam. She was certainly not the mastermind behind all of this. I knew better than anyone that contradicting my father was not an easy thing to do. As my body began to relax, I sat down beside her and let her take my hand.

"I want you to know that I never condoned what your father did," she told me. "Believe it or not, I actually like Jake. Regardless, I never spoke up when I should have and therefore I'm just as much to blame as he is. No one should have her choices taken away from her, and I will hold that guilt for the rest of my life because I saw what it did to you. Somehow, I let myself believe that he was doing what was best for you. I'm sorry, honey."

We sat there for a while, hand-in-hand, until my tears eventually subsided. I didn't offer any words of forgiveness or pretend like it was all okay – because it wasn't – and I don't think she expected me to say anything.

"Come with me," she stood, gesturing for me to follow her. "There's something I need to show you."

She led me into her bedroom and walked over to the dresser where her antique jewelry box sat prominently on top. Delicately lifting the lid, she reached inside and pulled out a small flat box, wrapped in silver wrapping paper. She handed it to me, and I saw that there was a note folded neatly and tucked under the ribbon.

"This is what Jake left for you. It should have been given to you four years ago, and I don't expect you to ever forgive us for keeping it from you, but it was meant for you and it's time you finally got it."

Taking a deep breath, I sat down on the edge of my mother's bed and ran my fingers over the smooth wrapping paper. I was in no way prepared for what might be inside, but I knew I needed to open it.

"Take your time," my mom said. "And when you're ready there's somewhere I want to take you."

I nodded, unable to peel my eyes away from the little box that held a piece of my past. A piece that had been taken from me. My mom walked out of the room and closed the door behind her, leaving me alone to uncover whatever was inside.

Carefully, I untied the ribbon and began to pull apart the silver wrapping, revealing a black gift box. My hands were shaking as I took the lid off and unfolded the tissue paper, revealing what was inside. Fresh tears immediately pooled in my eyes when I saw what it was.

It was a delicate sterling silver charm bracelet. I held it up to get a closer look, running my fingers over each tiny charm to see what he had chosen to put on it. There was a truck, a musical note, a guitar, a football, a rowboat and a heart. It was absolutely perfect. Jake had chosen charms that represented our time together, and each one held a million different memories that we had shared. Driving around in his old truck, all the times I sang for him and played guitar, watching him play in pickup football games, rowing around in the boat at his fishing cabin, and the heart... well, that one was pretty obvious.

It was the most amazing and thoughtful gift that I'd ever received. A fresh wave of anger and sadness ran through me when I thought about the fact that I should have gotten it four years ago, and I couldn't help but imagine how differently my life might have turned out if I had.

Finally, I reached for the folded note that I'd carefully put aside and began to unfold it. It was a sheet of white, lined paper that had been torn from a notebook, and I could see Jake's messy handwriting covering the page. I took a deep breath and read it.

Babe,

I know I'm going to see you in a few hours, but since you hate it when I buy you things I decided to drop this off so you would have no choice but to take it.

We've been telling ourselves that nothing's going to change when you leave, but let's face it ... we both know that it is. But it's okay. Change is good. You're starting a new, exciting chapter of your life and I'm so happy for you, 'cause you're gonna be amazing! I know you feel guilty for leaving me behind, but don't. I am with you no matter where you go.

But, since you are so stubborn and need more convincing, I got you this. This way, you are taking me and all our memories with you when you go. Just because you're leaving doesn't mean you're not taking your past (and me!) with you. Also, I expect you to fill it up with new memories from your awesome big city adventures.

You know I'm going to miss you like crazy, and it'll be hard, but I promise we'll be okay. My heart is with you, always. Besides,

I'm going to visit you so much that you'll be sick of me in no time!

I love you Nora Jane Montgomery. Can't wait to see you tonight.

-J

I read his note a half-dozen times until the paper was drenched in my own tears. I thought about how angry I was at Jake when he never showed up that day and guilt consumed me. How could I have let myself believe that he had just left me? He'd proven to me over and over again how much he loved me, and how much he cared for me. Then, when it was put to the test, I'd easily let myself think that he'd gone back his old womanizing ways and was done with me. How could I have believed that? I should have known better. When he didn't show up that day, I should have known that something was wrong, and done everything possible to find him. As much as I wanted to place all the blame on my parents, I knew that I couldn't. I should have trusted him and fought harder. Perhaps if I'd done that, I never would have lost him.

Once I'd calmed myself down, I found my mother and agreed to go with her to wherever it was that she felt she needed to take me. After a short time in the car, I saw that we were heading to Hilton Head Island.

"Are we going to Gramma's?" I asked. My grandmother, Edith, was my dad's mother, and the only grandparent I had left. My dad's father had died when he was a teenager, and my mom's parents had both passed away when I was young. I'd always been close with my Gramma Edith. When I was a kid, I'd stay with her at her house in Charleston whenever my parents went away, and even as I got older, I still would always take a week or so in the summer to spend time there with her. I hadn't come home to Beaufort at all during my four years of college, but I had been to Charleston. I'd even taken my roommate, Olivia, down there during spring vacation one year, and we'd stayed with my Gramma Edith. The three of us had so much fun together that Olivia had always begged to go again sometime.

My grandmother still had the house in Charleston, but nowadays she spent most of her time at her condo in Hilton Head. It had been a long time since I'd seen her so I was excited for the visit, I just didn't understand why she was the one my mom wanted to go see.

I was barely out of the car when my grandmother came bounding outside to greet me. Her short gray hair was impeccably styled, and she was wearing pristine white knee-length shorts and a pale pink polo, which meant she'd been out golfing that morning. Her age had never slowed her down for a minute.

"Nora, my beautiful girl! How are you?" She pulled me in for a big hug and kissed both my cheeks before we made our way inside.

"I'm okay," I responded, trying to feign enthusiasm. I hadn't seen her in ages, and it wasn't her fault that I was in a depressive slump.

"Oh, don't kid yourself, darling," she retorted. "Your mother already filled me in your situation, and there's no need to fake it around me."

I sat down in her exquisitely decorated, beach themed living room, surrounded by starfish and seashells, while she poured us iced tea, and I waited for them to explain why I was here.

Once our refreshments were poured, my grandmother finally sat down next to me. "Now dear, what your father did was inexcusable, I know that. But as awful as it was, he's not the monster that he seems, and there are a few things about his past that you should know. It won't excuse what he did, but it might help you understand why he is the way he is."

Intrigued, I remained quiet and let her continue.

"When your father was a kid, he was a lot like you. He was passionate, full of life and, believe it or not, he had a very artistic soul. He started playing the piano when he was about eight years old, and by age ten, he was permanently attached to his seat at the piano."

By now I was pretty sure that my jaw had dropped all the way to the carpet, but my grandmother just nodded and kept going with the story.

"His father, my husband, was working as a lawyer and spent nearly every waking hour at the office, which didn't leave him much time to spend with your father and me. It used to upset your father so much, but when he found the piano, it was like he'd found his niche in life and nothing else mattered. There were times, as he got older, that he would step back from his music or take a break for a little while, but he always found his way back. By the time he was a teenager, he knew he wanted to do it for the rest of his life. He wanted to study at Juilliard and become a concert pianist. He was good, too. I think he could have done it."

"So then what happened?" I asked.

"When your grandfather passed away, everything changed. All of a sudden, your dad felt like it was his responsibility to take care of us and fill his father's shoes. We didn't need the money – my husband and I both came from wealthy families, so we were always financially secure – but your dad was so determined. It was as though he felt that he owed it his father to follow in his footsteps. After that, he never played again."

"How did I not know about this?"

"Well, he never talks about it. I think it's painful for him. He completely left that part of himself behind, and I let him do it." There was pain and remorse etched in her soft features. "I have always regretted letting him throw away his dreams. I should have encouraged him to follow his heart and told him that his father would have been proud of him no matter what he chose to do. Unfortunately, I didn't. But I will not let you make the same mistake."

My grandmother reached over to grab my hand, her eyes wet with unshed tears. "Nora, you have a beautiful talent in music that will take you as far as you want to go with it. But I also know how hard you've worked to make your father happy and how important he is to you. I can see how torn you are and how unhappy it makes you. It's a big decision, and you need to choose what's right for *you*. You can't always make decisions with your head. There are times you have to listen to your heart and trust that it will steer you in the right direction. We don't always choose our path in life. Sometimes it chooses us. It might not be the smoothest ride, but you will end up where you're meant to be. Do what makes you happy, no matter what, and don't worry about the details. Details have a way of working themselves out in the end."

She squeezed my hand gently. "I love you, beautiful girl, and I want more than anything for you to be happy," she said. "Your father loves you, too, and he will be there for you no matter what. Now, as far as that boy of yours. Don't let your father stand in the way of what you have, because I know that you two have something special. I always did like him, even though you snuck out of my house in the middle of the night to go see him."

"You knew about that?" I gasped.

"Of course I knew!" she laughed. "He drove that old beat up pickup that sounded like a tractor backfiring. I could hear him as soon as he turned onto my street!"

My mom and I didn't talk much on the drive home, and my mind was still reeling from what my grandmother had told me. I felt like there was a whole different side to my father that I didn't even know. I always wondered why I was so musically inclined when no one else in my family ever was. Who would have thought that my love of music came from the one person who was so determined to keep me away from it?

It was dark when we arrived back at my parents' house. I quickly unbuckled my seatbelt and flung the door open, eager find Jake so we could talk some of this over.

"Nora, wait," my mom said, stopping me before I got out of the car. "I want you to know that I am behind you one hundred percent. No matter what happens with your father, I promise to support you this time. I love you, and this time I'm on your side."

"Thank you, Mom." I leaned over to give her a big hug before getting out of the car. I couldn't stay mad at her after what she'd done for me today. She didn't have to give me the present from Jake or take me to see my grandmother, but she had, and I was grateful.

As mind-boggling as the day had turned out, one thing was certain: I had some big decisions to make, and for the first time in my life, I was ready to make them on my own. Now that I had my mom and my grandmother in my corner supporting me, I wasn't alone anymore. I felt like I was finally free. My life and my choices belonged to me, and it was up to me to decide what to do with them.

I drove past my father's office on my way back to Jake's house and saw the lights on and his car still sitting in the parking lot. Surprisingly, I didn't have the same urge to talk to him as I had earlier. I wasn't scared anymore, but I felt like I needed to figure out a few things, and maybe try to come up with some kind of plan, before having that conversation.

I still couldn't believe that I'd never known about my father's past. I kept thinking back to my childhood, trying to remember a time that he had displayed even the slightest hint of his musical side and came up empty. I'd barely seen him even glance at the piano in the sitting room at my parents' house, and I had no memories of him ever playing it. I'd always assumed that the piano was just a prop or a conversation piece that my parents kept as yet another symbol of their wealth. Turns out it was actually a piece of his childhood. An important piece.

What bewildered me most was that my father had completely shut himself off from his music, permanently. No matter what path I took, I couldn't imagine my life without music in it. Did he regret his decisions, or was he happier now? Would I eventually be happy if I made the same choices he did?

Jake's truck wasn't in the driveway when I pulled up, and none of the lights were on in his apartment. I hoped that he would be home soon because I really needed to talk to him. I fished his spare key out from under the mat on his front porch and let myself inside.

I flipped on the lights and saw that the house was empty. No Max, and no Jake. Exhausted, I settled down on the couch and waited for him to get home. It had been a long, emotional day, and once I got comfortable on the couch, I had a hard time keeping my eyes open. Finally, I covered myself with a blanket and gave in to my exhaustion, hoping that Jake would see me here when he got home and wake me up so we could talk.

My eyes fluttered open when I felt something cool and wet on my cheek. I was greeted by Max sniffing my face and rapidly wagging his tail. The sunshine pouring in through the windows indicated that it was late morning, and I wondered why Jake hadn't woken me up when he got in.

"Gosh, Nora, I'm so sorry. I didn't realize you were here!" Jake's mother came around the corner, looking surprised to see me as she pulled Max away from me.

Embarrassed, I stood up and tried to smooth out my wrinkled clothing. "Hi, Mrs. Harris, I'm sorry. I was waiting for Jake to come home last night and I must have fallen asleep."

"Oh, honey, he and Ethan decided to head down to Charleston early. He dropped Max off at the house yesterday, and I just came by to pick up the dog food. Is everything okay?"

Disappointment rushed through me. "Oh, okay. No, no, everything's fine. I just wanted to talk to him."

She sat down on the couch, a knowing expression on her face, and patted the cushion next to her, encouraging me to sit down. "Don't worry, Nora, you two will work it all out. Jake may be stubborn as a mule, but that boy loves you and would do anything for you."

"Yeah, I know he would." I managed a small smile.

"He was going to try and pick up a new phone when he got there, so you should be able to get in touch with him later today or tomorrow."

"Thank you, Mrs. Harris," I said gratefully. "I really appreciate it."

"Honey, please, you know you can call me Eileen. I've missed you around here, and I keep telling Jake to bring you over to the house, but of course he just wants to keep you all to himself. Maybe when you get back from the wedding, I can convince him to bring you over for dinner."

"I would love that," I said. "I've missed you too, Eileen."

She gave me a quick hug before I made my way out the door. I didn't realize how much I'd missed her. She'd been like a second mother to me when I was in high school, and often times I had an easier time going to her for advice than my actual mother.

"Oh, and Nora," she called to me as I was stepping outside. "Just so you know, he turned the job down." Before I had a chance to respond, she was already in the other room. I should have guessed that she knew everything that was going on between her son and me. She could read Jake like a book, and he'd never been able to keep anything from her.

After leaving Jake's, I went back to my parents' house to pack for Charleston. I was heading there tomorrow with Susie and the other bridesmaids for a little R&R before the wedding. I was still upset that I hadn't gotten to see Jake before he left, and I hoped he hadn't left early because he was still angry with me. Even though we would both be in Charleston, I knew that all the pre-wedding activities and preparation would take up most of our time, and I likely wouldn't have many opportunities to see him.

I felt my phone vibrating from inside my purse, and when I looked at the screen, I saw that I had a bunch of missed calls and voicemails. I hoped that Jake had gotten a new phone and tried to call, but when I scrolled through the list, the only name I saw was Susie's. I clicked on the most recent voicemail to listen to her message.

"Nora Montgomery! Where are you chica? It's wedding crunch time and my maid of honor has gone MIA! I'm sitting here with half a dozen sexy lingerie sets in front of me, and I need you to get your kinky ass over here and help me choose one for my wedding night. Call me back, bitch! Love you."

Laughing to myself, I immediately made a beeline for Susie's house. I hadn't been a very good maid of honor, and I felt terrible that I'd been neglecting her when she needed me. From now on I would give her my full attention. Besides, if there was anyone in the world who could take my mind off everything that was going on in my life, it was my best friend.

Jake

You know how they say that a watched pot never boils? Well, apparently all that shit is actually true.

I had spent the last few weeks staring at my phone waiting to hear back about my job interview in Charleston, and naturally, it wasn't until I smashed my phone into smithereens that they ended up calling.

Just my luck.

After my argument with Nora, followed by my confrontation with her father, I decided it was probably best for me to get a little space. I needed to chill out and regain some perspective. I convinced Ethan to head to Charleston a few days early so we could squeeze in some extra "guy time" before the wedding. Not only did it give me a chance to get my head together, but it also conveniently got Ethan away from Susie while she was in bridezilla mode. I knew that Susie would fill Nora in on the plan, and I hoped she wouldn't feel like I was running away from her. Although, in some ways, I guessed I was.

When I finally picked up a new phone, I turned it on and saw that I had a voicemail waiting for me from Jason Tredwell about the project in Charleston. He wanted to arrange a second interview, and since I was already in town, we got together and went over some of the finer details of the project. We ended up talking for a few hours and it seemed to have gone really well. He loved my ideas and told me that I was one of three people who were being considered for the job, but I still wouldn't allow myself to get my hopes up. It seemed like a long shot that they would choose to hire me when the other two architects probably had far more experience.

The two other groomsmen in Ethan's wedding party, Andy and Chris, had already arrived in Charleston, so no one had noticed when I slipped away for a few hours to go to the meeting. Andy was one of our closest friends growing up, and Chris had been Ethan's college roommate. I didn't know him all that well, but he seemed like a good guy, and we'd always gotten along.

I knew that Nora and Susie were also in Charleston by now, but our groups were staying in different hotels for the first part of the week until the rehearsal dinner. The girls were busy doing whatever girly stuff women do before a wedding, while we occupied ourselves with fishing, drinking, and other guy stuff.

Still, despite all the fun we were having during our "bachelor week," I already found myself missing Nora. We hadn't spoken all week, and I needed to know if she was still upset with me. Tomorrow night was the rehearsal dinner. I didn't want things to be awkward between us, so I decided to send her a brief text just so she would know I was still thinking about her. Hopefully her response, or lack of response, would give me a better idea of where we stood. I decided to keep it simple and typed a quick message.

Can't wait 2 see u

Several minutes went by with no response, and I began to worry. I had let nearly the whole week go by without contacting her, so there was a good chance she hated me by now.

Fuck!

Just as I was about to flee my hotel room so I could find her and do some damage control, my phone buzzed with a new message.

Me either :)

Relief flooded through me, and I relaxed back on the bed. Nora knew me better than anyone, which meant she knew my moods well enough to know that even though pulling away was my knee-jerk reaction to conflict, it didn't mean that I was actually gone. I knew we had to talk, but I didn't want things to be too tense between us. She seemed to feel the same way. This week was about having fun and celebrating our best friends getting married. I didn't want anything to get in the way of that. Whatever issues we needed to work out could be put on hold until we got back.

The day of the rehearsal dinner, all the groomsmen and the groom moved over to the hotel where the rest of the wedding party was staying and where the dinner was taking place. By the time dinner rolled around, I was settled in, showered, and dressed in my best black suit with a crisp, white dress shirt.

We made our way down to the restaurant bar where we would meet the rest of the wedding party, along with Susie and Ethan's families. Naturally the girls were fashionably late, so by the time they arrived I had already finished half my drink, which had done nothing to settle my nerves.

My eyes settled on Nora as soon as she walked in the room, looking as gorgeous as ever in a short, tight gold and silver dress. I wasted no time before going over to her. She was chatting with one of the other bridesmaids, but when she saw me approaching, she smiled and politely excused herself.

"I'm sorry," I said as soon as I was close enough for her to hear me.

"No, I'm sorry," she replied. "I can't believe my father did that."

"It's not your fault," I said, shaking my head. "I was never mad at you, and I shouldn't have run off like I did. I was just... frustrated."

"I know. I got to do a lot of thinking though, and there's a lot of stuff I want to talk to you about."

"It can wait," I interrupted her. "For now, let's just enjoy this weekend together. I know you have a lot to think about and we some big decisions to make, but I don't want to rush you. We have plenty of time to talk about this later, so let's just enjoy ourselves for now, okay?"

"Okay," she agreed, a smile returning to her face.

"God, I missed you." I pulled her into me, forgetting about everything else as soon as my lips brushed against hers, and relishing the way she felt in my arms. It took all the restraint I had to keep myself from dragging her up to my room and burying myself deep inside her.

Her cheeks flushed as though she could read my mind. "I missed you, too."

Throughout the entire dinner, as Nora and I snuck glances at each other across the table, all I could think about was getting out of there. I couldn't wait to bring her upstairs and peel that sexy little dress off her.

Unfortunately, the bride and groom had other plans. They didn't want the festivities to end, and since they couldn't see each other until tomorrow's ceremony, our two groups continued the night by going in separate directions.

Nora shot me a disappointed look as she turned to follow Susie and the other girls to a club down the street. I watched her walk away for a moment, until I was forced in the opposite direction to join Ethan and the guys, who were already halfway down the block on the way to another bar. As much as I hated having to postpone my night with Nora, I knew Ethan would never forgive me if I abandoned him on his last night as a bachelor, so I put on my game face and ran to catch up with him.

I wasn't planning on drinking too much, but I realized early on that the guys had other ideas. As soon as I finished one drink, someone was putting another one in my hand. The pattern continued all night and before I knew it, I was plastered.

Attempting to sober myself up, I stood at the bar and asked the bartender for a tall glass of water. As I was chugging it down I felt two small hands on my waist and spun around, hoping to see Nora. It was just my luck that instead of being greeted by a beautiful brunette, I was faced with an aggressive blonde.

"Lindsey," I grumbled, not bothering to hide my irritation. "What are you doing here?"

"Looking for you." She pushed herself into me, pinning me against the bar. "Ethan said you were here."

"Thanks a lot, Ethan." I tried to maneuver myself around her, but my drunken body couldn't seem to push through the people who were packed around me.

"Aw, come on, baby." she reached her hands under my shirt and trailed them up my back, arching her breasts into me. "You know you want to."

I shoved her hands off and glared down at her. "No, actually I don't. Cut the shit and leave me alone. I'm not interested. I'm in love with Nora."

"Oh, please," she scoffed. "When will you realize that you'll never be good enough for that little princess? She may be into you now, but her family will never accept you, and she'll end up kicking your ass to the curb. If you think she'll actually choose you over her family then you're stupider than I thought. People like us don't end up with people like her. The sooner you accept that, the better."

Lindsey had struck a nerve, but there was no way I was going to let it show. I'd had enough of people telling me who I could and couldn't be with.

"You don't know shit," I snapped. "Now get the hell out of my way." My anger had sobered me up enough to get around her and find my way through the crowd. I said a quick goodbye to Ethan and then got the hell out of there.

As soon as I got back to my room at the hotel, I stripped down to my boxers and about to climb into bed when I heard a knock on the door.

Great, first she corners me at the bar, and now she's stalking me in the hotel.

"I told you I'm not interested, Lindsey," I called out, stomping over to the door and flinging it open. "Get it through your–"

I stopped when I saw that it wasn't Lindsey on the other side of my door. This time, it was someone I actually wanted to see. She was in a white, fluffy hotel robe and had an adorably flirty grin on her face.

"Is this a bad time?" Nora said, toying with the lapels of her robe to give me a peek at the black lace she was wearing underneath.

I stood in the doorway, frozen in place, and gaped at the goddess standing in front of me until I finally managed to choke out a response.

"Hell no, baby." I wrapped my arms around her, taking her mouth in a fierce kiss as I pulled her into my room and slammed the door behind us.

As my lips moved furiously against hers, my hands were pulling at the material of her robe, eager to see what she had on underneath. Nora grabbed my hands, gently pushing me to sit on the edge of the bed while she stood in front of me. Taking a step back so we were no longer touching, she slowly tugged the cord of her robe to untie it and then let it slide off her shoulders, revealing the black lace lingerie she had on underneath.

My mouth fell open, and I was rendered speechless as I let my eyes wander over her body, taking in every sexy inch of her. Her breasts swelled over the sheer black lace babydoll, which split open in the front over her tan, flat stomach and fell to her hips where the matching barely-there panties peeked out from underneath. By now all my blood had moved to my dick, and it was so hard I could probably cut diamonds with it. All I wanted to do was touch her, but she stayed just out of reach – teasing me and letting me take it all in.

"What do you think?" she said, slowly spinning around to give me a good look. The sheer, delicate lace fell partially over her backside, but I could see the lines of her G-string and every curve of her perfect cheeks.

Holy shit.

"You're fucking perfect," I choked out, hardly able to speak. I'd never been so turned on in my entire life.

When she took a step toward me I didn't hesitate before reaching out and running my hands slowly up the back of her legs. I trailed them over her silky smooth skin and gripped her beautiful ass in my eager palms. I traced my finger along the edges of her tiny panties, landing between her legs where I could feel how wet she already was.

Nora moaned, pushing me down onto the mattress and then climbed over me, meeting her mouth with mine as she straddled my rock hard length between her legs. I cradled her bare ass in my hands and pulled her against me, making a soft wail escape her lips. She rocked over me, sliding her hot center along the hard ridge of my cock, and getting me so worked up that I knew it would be over soon if I didn't slow things down. As badly as I wanted to be inside of her, I wanted to draw this out a little longer and appreciate every second.

I rolled over and took Nora with me, laying her on her back as I settled between her legs. She ran her hands up my back, pulling me closer as she tightened her legs around my waist and rubbed her body against me. I trailed my lips down her jaw and along her neck to her collarbone, running my palm up her thigh and over her ribs until I reached her breast. She arched into my touch as I kneaded her breast through the thin fabric of her lingerie.

Moving my mouth downward, I kissed the swell of her breasts as her chest began to rise and fall and her breathing got heavier. My lips traveled the path of her cleavage as I slid my body down hers, pushing the delicate lace aside to continue my path of kisses over her stomach. I kissed and caressed every inch of her, worshipping her body and savoring every inch of her.

I kneeled up and began sliding her panties down her legs, pulling them off and tossing them to the side. My kisses continued up her leg until I reached the apex of her thighs and settled my mouth over her slick heat, softly pleasuring her with my lips and tongue until she began to cry out.

Just as I could feel her release building, she leaned forward and pulled me on top of her.

"I want you inside of me, Jake. Please."

Her eyes were burning with the same desire that I felt and I couldn't wait any longer. I stripped off my boxers and positioned myself over her. After carefully untying the ribbon at the front of her top, I pushed the lace aside to expose her full, perfect tits. My gaze fell hungrily on her taut nipples, and I couldn't resist covering them with my mouth before moving my lips back up to meet hers.

As I held myself over her and looked down into her beautiful green eyes, my feelings for her were overwhelming. I only hoped that she could see in my expression what I was unable to say in words. Finally I sank inside her, tantalizingly slowly, relishing in the way she felt.

"Ohmygod, Jake..." she breathed out.

I moved deep inside, keeping a slow pace as I slid in and out while she moaned in pleasure and clawed at my back, her legs tightening around me like a vice.

"You feel so fucking amazing, Nora. I will never get enough of this."

Her heels dug into my backside, desperately pulling me close. "Faster, Jake. Faster. I need you."

Gradually I picked up the pace, hooking my arm under her knee as I moved faster and harder inside her. She felt so fucking good, and I knew I wasn't going to last much longer, but I didn't care. As soon as I felt her begin to tense around me, I pounded into her as hard and as deep as I could until she screamed out my name in her release. Letting myself go, I thrust into her one more time before joining her with a deep groan.

Exhausted, I pulled her back against my chest and drew the covers over us. Before falling asleep I moved my lips to her ear, no longer able to contain my feelings for her. I wanted her to know where I stood and how I felt, but when I opened my mouth those three words got stuck in my throat.

chapter thirteen

Nora

We woke up tangled around each other the next morning, both in a blissful haze after the amazing night we spent together. As much as I wanted to stay in bed, and go for round two, Jake hopped up, pulling me with him, and told me he wanted to show me something before we each went our separate ways to get ready for the ceremony.

After making a quick stop in my room to throw on some clean clothes, we grabbed two coffees from the hotel lobby and headed outside. It was warm and beautiful, an ideal day for a wedding.

I glanced around the hotel parking lot. "Where's your truck parked?"

"We're walking," Jake said, grabbing my hand. "Don't worry, it's not far."

We strolled along the waterfront on East Battery Street, enjoying the quiet that only came in the early morning before people began flooding into town. This was one of my favorite places to walk in Charleston, with the glassy ocean on one side and beautiful historic homes and towering palms lining the street on the other. I'd never seen it so serene and peaceful. Aside from a few joggers out on their morning run and the occasional car heading into town, we practically had the place to ourselves.

Jake led me through White Point Gardens and up a quiet side street until we were standing in front of a very old, very run-down building that looked like its best years were most definitely behind it. Still, despite the sagging porch and chipping paint, I could see how beautiful it had once been. I turned to look at Jake, waiting for him to explain why we were here.

"This is one of the oldest original homes here in Charleston," he told me, staring up at the sprawling building. "Almost all the homes that were built during that time have been renovated or re-modeled, but this one is practically untouched. Aside from a few band-aids and superficial repairs over the years, it stands exactly as it did when it was built."

"Wow, I'm surprised it's still standing."

"The structure itself is still pretty solid, that's the beauty about these historic buildings. They were constructed during a time when homes were built to last centuries rather than just a few decades. They didn't cut corners to save time and money like people do to-day. They built homes that would be around to pass down to their families through the generations. Unfortunately, today they just don't build them like they used to."

"So, what's going to happen with this place?"

"Well, this is the project that I interviewed for. The one that I *really* want. The owners want to completely restore it, down to every last detail, and bring it back to its former glory. It's a historic site, which requires that some part of the original structure needs to remain and be used in the new structure. Normally, people just keep a couple of windows or the front door, and then re-create eve-rything else using new materials because it's easier and faster than trying to restore the other parts of the building."

"But that's not what you would do?"

He shook his head. "What I proposed was to restore and reuse as much of the original building as possible, like the columns on the front porch, the tiles on the roof, the beautiful crown molding, and of course the windows and doors. They would be as good as new after being restored, and there's no way to replicate those original details using today's materials. It would just be a cheap knock-off. With my plan I would integrate the old with the new, bringing the past and the present together."

I was completely blown away by how incredibly passionate and knowledgeable he was. I was seeing him in an entirely new light. This was a side of him that I'd never known before, and I loved it.

"What did they think of your ideas?" I asked.

"They seemed to like the plan I proposed, but it all comes down to how much time and money the owners are willing to put into it." He sighed, looking over at the house he was so clearly passionate about. "They would be taking a risk on me, and they might decide to go with someone more conventional who has more experience."

"You're worth the risk, Jake." I looked up at him and squeezed his hand in mine. "They would be crazy not to choose you, and I'm not just saying that because you rocked my world last night."

He laughed, leaning down to give me a quick kiss before we turned to go back to the hotel. I was so glad he'd brought me to the house and showed me that side of him. After all this time, it was nice to know that there were still things to learn about each other.

As we walked back to the hotel, Jake pointed out different aspects and features of some of the old homes that we passed along the way. I enjoyed seeing him in his element. I could have spent the entire day with him just walking around the city and learning more about what he did. Unfortunately this was the calm before the storm, and when we got back to the hotel we would be faced with the chaos of getting ready for Susie and Ethan's big day.

When we arrived back at the hotel, Jake walked me to my room before we parted ways.

"Try to keep the bride from going too crazy, okay?" he said with a wink as he walked away. "I'll see you on your way down the aisle."

Things were in full swing when I entered Susie's suite to meet up with her and the other bridesmaids. After making a quick phone call to the wedding planner, who confirmed that everything was right on track and going smoothly, I decided it was time to start getting ready.

Donning our matching bride/bridesmaid sweat suits, we got our hair and makeup done while sipping on mimosas and waited until it was time to put our dresses on. I couldn't help but notice that Susie seemed unusually calm for a woman who was walking down the aisle in a few hours' time.

"How ya doin, Sus?" I asked her.

"Fine and dandy, my friend! Ready to get this show on the road though so I can finally be Mrs. Ethan Burke!"

Kate and Mindy were hooting and hollering from their makeup stations, and I just laughed. Most brides would be running around like crazy to make sure everything was perfect, or worrying whether or not the groom-to-be had run off somewhere with cold feet, but Susie was relaxing on the couch and sipping her mimosa without a care in the world. If it were anyone else I might search her bag for pills or administer a breathalyzer test, but this was typical Susie – she had worked her butt off to plan every detail of the wedding perfectly, but then when the time came to really start stressing out, she just said "Screw it" and stopped worrying or caring about the details.

Susie and Ethan were so sure about each other and so eager to devote their lives to one another. For them, there was never a question about whether or not they would end up together because they'd always seemed to know, even at the beginning. I admired that about them, and I wondered if I would ever have that feeling of absolute certainty. Perhaps I already had it, but hadn't let myself believe it or trust in it.

Jake

"So, am I supposed to give you some kind of pep talk and make sure you don't have cold feet or whatever?" I asked. Ethan and I were lounging in the outdoor bar at the hotel, drinking beers with Chris and Andy until it was time to get changed.

"Hell, no!" Ethan exclaimed. "I'm about to marry the girl of my dreams. I've been waiting for this day since I was eighteen. Time to get the party started!"

"All right dude, let's do it," I said with a laugh.

Once we had changed into our wedding attire – a gray suit and matching vest with a mint colored tie—we loaded into the car and made the five-minute drive to the wedding venue. It was a big historic home downtown with a large outdoor space and beautiful gardens where the ceremony would be held. There was an outdoor terrace that had been tented for the reception, and several tables were set up inside for dining. It just so happened that the house had been built in 1825 and was well known for its architectural importance, so naturally I couldn't help but admire it. I was a nerd when it came to architecture.

We waited in one of the upstairs rooms and watched through the bay window as the guests arrived and began filling the wooden chairs around the floral arch, which would serve as a makeshift altar where they would be exchanging vows. A beautiful three-tiered antique fountain served as a backdrop for the ceremony, and flowers covered nearly every surface. I didn't care much about decorations and all that shit, but even I had to admit that it was pretty damn nice.

When it was almost time to begin, the wedding planner ushered us downstairs and directed us to our positions at the altar where the minister stood waiting. I did a quick check to make sure the ring was still safely tucked away in my pocket before following Ethan down the aisle and taking my place beside him. Chris and Andy stood on my other side as we waited until the processional music began to play.

Everyone went silent and turned in their seats to watch the bride's approach. Everyone except for me. I was looking for Nora.

From around the corner came Ethan's little niece, the flower girl, who was haphazardly throwing flower petals out of a small basket as she made her way down the aisle. Following closely behind her were the other two bridesmaids, and finally Nora.

My eyes locked onto her and everything else faded into the background. Susie could have been walking down the aisle wearing nothing but a smile, and I wouldn't have had any idea. All I saw was Nora. Her long dress flowed around her like the angel she was, and her dazzling smile lit up my heart. When her eyes met mine, I think my knees actually went weak. I couldn't help the huge grin that spread across my face.

Susie arrived in front of the minister, and I gave Ethan an encouraging pat on the back as they met each other in the middle. As hard as I tried to devote my attention to the ceremony, I couldn't take my eyes off Nora. Every once in a while her gaze would drift to meet mine, and I could see the faint blush rise in her cheeks as we stared meaningfully at each other from opposite sides of the altar. I only hoped that she was feeling the same things I was.

Ethan and Susie began reading the vows that they had written themselves. It was hard not to get caught up in the emotion that went along with the promises they made to each other. I could see Nora's eyes fill with tears as she watched our best friends devote themselves to one another. What they had was so special and uncomplicated. I envied that.

When it was time for them to exchange rings, I carefully pulled Susie's diamond band out of my pocket and handed it to

Ethan, while Nora did the same with Ethan's simple platinum band. When the minister pronounced them husband and wife, they joined in a passionate kiss while everyone cheered them on.

Holding my arm out for Nora, I led her down the aisle as we followed Susie and Ethan out through the crowd of people. We joined the rest of the wedding party for the photos, posing for the photographer until my cheeks were sore from smiling.

By the time we rejoined the guests at the reception, the sun was just beginning to set, creating a picturesque background of oranges, yellows, and pinks. The area outside had been transformed into a wonderland of hanging lanterns and twinkling lights. Guests mingled until it was time to be seated at the tables inside so that the bride and groom could make their grand entrance.

I picked up drinks for Nora and myself as I made my way to the head table, but Nora wasn't there. By now everyone was seated, and just as I was about to sneak off to try and find her, I heard her voice over the loudspeaker.

"Ladies and Gentleman, allow me to introduce for the first time, Mr. and Mrs. Ethan Burke!"

Everyone cheered as Ethan and Susie entered the room, their hands raised together in the air and matching hundred watt smiles on their faces as they made their way to the middle of the dance floor. Nora was standing on the small stage in front of the microphone stand holding her guitar and looking as nervous as I'd ever seen her.

"As Susie's maid of honor, I'm supposed to make a toast," Nora said into the mic. "But, since I'm terrible at public speaking, I decided to give in to her much less nerve-wracking request to sing for their first dance."

Nora settled onto the stool and began strumming the first notes of "If I Didn't Have You" by Thompson Square, as Susie and Ethan began slow dancing while all the guests looked on. As nervous as Nora had looked when she started, by the time she reached the first chorus she was completely in her element. Her voice was velvety smooth and hit each note perfectly. When the song was finished and the crowd cheered, I think it was just as much for her as it was for the newlyweds. Blushing nervously, she climbed off the stage and sat down next to me at the table.

I leaned over, getting close enough that my lips brushed her skin, and whispered in her ear, "Incredible job, baby." Her blush deepened as she smiled back at me.

Champagne flutes were distributed as the bride and groom sat down, indicating it was time for the toasts to start. Grabbing my glass, I stood up and waited for the room to get quiet before I began.

"Hey folks, I'm Ethan's best man, Jake. I met Ethan on the first day of kindergarten when we fought over a toy truck at recess, and things escalated pretty quickly. It wasn't long before we were rolling around in the dirt and throwing punches at each other. By the time the teachers pried us apart, we had already done about as much damage as two scraggly five year olds could do, so naturally, we spent the rest of the day in time-out. However, at some point during the day we bonded over our even more intense mutual hatred for another kid in class, and by the end of the day, we'd forgotten that we were supposed to enemies. From that day forward we were best friends, partners in crime and thick as thieves.

"Girls eventually came into the picture, but things remained the same; we were still each other's number one. That is, until a certain blonde-haired beauty walked into our calculus class senior year. Susie here was the only junior in a class full of seniors, but she strolled into the classroom like she owned the damn place. Fearless, confident, hilarious. Man, all the girls hated her. Ethan's jaw was plastered to the floor, and ten minutes into the class he turned around and said to me, 'I think I'm in love with that girl.' Naturally, I ignored him.

"Finally, at the end of the semester, he got his chance. There was a review session after school for the calculus exam, and they both stayed for it. Now, I'm sure you have all heard the romantic tale of how they met – Susie was stranded in the parking lot when her car wouldn't start, and Ethan swooped in to save the day and offered her a ride home. After which the rest was history. However, what only Ethan and I know is that while they were studying away inside the classroom, I was in the parking lot removing the spark plug from Susie's engine."

The guests erupted in laughter, and Susie's mouth was wide open in shock while Ethan chuckled next to her.

"I figured they would go out for a while, and then Ethan would get sick of her and move on to someone else. However, when they hit the two-week mark, which was the usual expiration date for our relationships, instead of telling me that they were breaking up, Ethan looked at me and said, 'Dude, I'm gonna marry that girl.' I still didn't believe him, but that was the time when everything started to change. I went from being Ethan's number one to his number two, and all of a sudden I found myself home alone on Friday nights, playing video games by myself while Ethan and Susie were living out their fairytale. And even though it meant sharing my best bro, I would take that spark plug out all over again, because I'm honored to say that I had a role in helping Ethan find his soul mate."

Reaching into my pocket, I looked over at Susie and held up the spark plug that I'd stolen from her car all those years ago. "I never really knew why I kept this, but I guess some part of me must have known that you weren't just any girl. You were his forever."

I handed the spark plug to Susie, who looked like she might cry at any moment, and raised my glass in the air. "To Ethan and Susie – may you always be best friends, partners in crime, and thick as thieves!"

chapter fourteen

Nora

Jake and I were out on the dance floor, moving slowly to the music with our arms wrapped carefully around each other. It was the first time since that morning that we'd been able to spend any time together.

"Did you really think they would end up getting married?" I asked.

"I don't know," he shrugged. "I think I knew that they had something special, but when you're that young, you usually do something stupid to mess it up somehow. They managed to beat the odds."

For about the millionth time I wondered to myself where we would be if things hadn't gotten messed up between us the first time. "But do you think it will last? I mean, they've never been with anyone else. How can they know for sure? What if they eventually get bored with each other?"

"Because, when you know, you know. You stop noticing anyone else." He pulled back slightly and gazed down at me, reassuring me with the confidence I saw in his eyes. "And they won't get bored with each other because when you find your right person, everything becomes exciting. Even the most mundane things are interesting when you experience it with the person who sets your world on fire."

In that moment, standing in his strong arms, the decision was simple. All I wanted to do was tell him how I felt and where I stood. I needed him to know that I wanted to be with him, and only him.

"Jake, I have to–"

Just then a voice came over the loudspeaker, cutting me off and announcing that it was time for all the single ladies to gather for the tossing of the bouquet.

"You better get out there," Jake said, releasing me from his hold. "Fight hard for it baby," he winked, before sauntering off to watch us ladies battle it out.

I stood off to the side of the mob of single women, not wanting to get my dress torn or my eyes clawed out by any of the gung-ho women who looked like they were ready for combat. Susie gave me a conspiratorial smile before turning around and sure enough, when she tossed the bouquet over her shoulder, it magically found its way into my hands.

"Yay! Looks like you're next, Nora!" Susie cheered, clapping her hands together.

"Could you be any more obvious?" I laughed. "You might as well have just walked over and handed it to me!"

"I have no idea what you're talking about," she said, feigning innocence before grabbing Ethan and hauling him back out on the dance floor.

I scanned the room for Jake, hoping to get some time alone with him so I could talk to him, but I couldn't find him among the throngs of people inside. After grabbing a glass of water from the bar, I went outside to the porch to get some fresh air and think about how I would break my news to Jake. Hopefully he would be so excited that he'd whisk me away to his room, and we would spend the rest of the night celebrating my decision. Then we could finally relax and enjoy our lives together. That was what he wanted… right?

I was over-thinking things again. Of course that's what Jake wanted. Just because we hadn't discussed where our relationship was headed didn't mean that he wasn't invested in building a future with me. I mean, he wouldn't let me make such a life-altering change if he wasn't fully committed, would he? He hadn't said out loud that he loved me, but I'd assumed it was just because he was waiting until we had things figured out.

My thoughts were interrupted when I heard someone coming up behind me. When I turned around and saw Lindsey, my body immediately tensed.

"Nice bouquet," she scoffed. "Looks like you're all ready to ride off into the sunset with Jake."

I rolled my eyes. "What goes on with me and Jake is none of your damn business."

"Well, I hate to be the one to break it to you, but Jake is no prince charming and your little fairy tale isn't going to end with a happily ever after. Now that he's finally had you, it's only a matter of time before he gets bored and comes crawling back to me for another wild roll in the sheets."

I'd had enough of this bitch. She didn't know the real Jake, and she sure as hell didn't know how we felt about each other. I wasn't going to let her get under my skin and make me question our relationship. I was sick and tired of people trying to come between us.

"I hate to be the one to break it to *you*, Lindsey, but you were nothing more than a drunken mistake. A sad, easy substitute for the one who he actually wanted. Me. He never wanted you, and he never will want you. The sooner you get that through your head, the sooner you will stop embarrassing yourself. Jake is mine. Get over it and move on."

Her jaw had dropped, and for once she was actually speechless. Before she had a chance to come up with a retort, Jake came around the corner.

"Couldn't have said it any better myself." He grinned, dropping a quick kiss on my lips before turning to Lindsey. "Get out of here and leave us the hell alone."

Jake

When I'd seen Lindsey head off in Nora's direction, I knew immediately that she was going to cause trouble. I'd been about a half second away from jumping in to defend Nora, but when she fired back that perfect response, I realized that she was more than capable of holding her own. I was still smiling at her words, and I was glad that she hadn't believed any of the bullshit that had come pouring out of Lindsey's mouth. She had confidence in me.

As soon as Lindsey had stormed off, I turned to Nora with a huge grin. "So... I'm yours, eh?"

"Yup," she smiled. "You're mine, and I'm yours. Got a problem with that?"

"Absolutely not," I said, wrapping my arms around her. "No problem with that whatsoever."

She tucked her body against mine, where she fit perfectly. "Good."

"I'm sorry that you had to deal with her, and I hope you know that there was no truth to what she said. She doesn't know anything about how I feel about you."

"So you're not going to get bored with me?"

Nora said it in a teasing way, but I could see the flicker of uncertainty in her eyes and I was determined to extinguish it for good.

"Never in a million years," I replied easily, pulling her close and placing a gentle kiss in her hair. "Do you want to get out of here?"

"Yes, please. It's been a long day and all I can think about is a nice, hot shower. We should probably say goodbye to Susie and

Ethan first, though."

"Okay, let's go." I took her hand and we went in search of the newlyweds. The crowd had thinned out substantially, and it seemed like the party was dying down. We said a quick goodbye to the bride and groom, promising to see them off tomorrow morning when they left for their honeymoon, and then made our way out.

Lined up in the circular driveway in front of the house were three horse-drawn carriages that Susie had arranged to bring guests who were staying in town back to their hotels. The large group in front of us occupied the first two, so Nora and I hopped into the third one, and I directed the driver where to take us.

I saw Nora shiver in the cool night air, so I wrapped my jacket around her shoulders and pulled her close to keep her warm. It was a beautiful night, and the sound of the horse's hooves against the pavement made a *clip, clop* rhythm that nearly put me to sleep. The whole day had been amazing, up until the confrontation with Lindsey, and I hated that she had tarnished an otherwise flawless time.

Nora was quiet during the ride back to the hotel. Even though she'd told me that she was okay, I still worried that she might be upset about what Lindsey had said. I walked her up to her room and paused outside the door when she pushed it open, unsure of whether or not she wanted me to join her.

She looked at me questioningly when I hung back. "Aren't you coming in?"

"I wasn't sure if you wanted to be alone."

"Don't be silly. Get in here." She smiled, grabbing me by the shirt and pulling me inside.

I found a small bottle of whiskey in the mini-bar and poured us both a drink. Before we drank, Nora held her glass up to propose a toast.

"To that crazy-ass Lindsey! Let's hope that now she'll finally set her sights on someone else."

"I already feel bad for whoever that poor sucker is," I chuckled.

We laughed and clinked our glasses together before taking a drink. The whiskey ran down my throat with a comforting burn that warmed my stomach and instantly relaxed me. Still, there was something plaguing me, and I needed to get it off my chest.

"Nora, I should never have let this thing with Lindsey get this far. I should have told her off a long time ago, and I didn't. I was trying to be sensitive to the fact that she's Ethan's cousin, and by doing that, she wound up hurting you, and I hate myself for that. As much as I loved seeing you tell her off... because that was sexy as hell... you shouldn't have had to do it at all. I'm so sorry, baby."

Nora smiled. "Thank you, but it's okay. I promise. I've wanted to give that girl a piece of my mind since I was seventeen. I think it was actually kind of therapeutic. But, now I plan on hopping in the shower and putting all that drama behind me."

She went into the bathroom and turned on the shower. I loosened my tie and pulled it off, eager to finally get out of my suit. Before I could finish undressing, Nora called me into the bathroom.

"Can you help me unzip my dress?" she asked with a playful smile. Turning around, she pulled her hair to the side so I could access the zipper. My fingers grazed her smooth back as I pulled it down, itching to get her dress off and touch every inch of her.

As she spun around to face me, she let her dress fall to the floor and pressed up against me. "Did I mention how sexy you are in that suit?" Nora looked up at me, her eyes burning with desire as she reached out and began unbuttoning my shirt.

My breathing got heavier. "I'll wear a suit every damn day if you want me to."

She pushed my shirt off my shoulders and let it fall to the floor. "I especially like knowing what's hidden underneath," she whispered in a sexy, seductive tone.

Her bare breasts grazed my chest and the hard points of her nipples caressed my skin, rendering me utterly speechless and incapable of coherent thought.

"Oh yeah?" I managed to choke out. All my blood had rushed south and was now pressing against the zipper of my dress pants.

Nora reached down and unbuckled my belt, letting her hand brush up against my firm cock as she freed it from its polyester cage. "Yeah," she purred, her soft breath tickling my chest. "And I like being the one that gets to unwrap it."

Unable to contain myself any longer, I hauled her into my arms and met her lips for a deep kiss. Once we'd stripped each other of our remaining clothes, I lifted her up and pulled her into the cascading stream of the shower. We lathered each other with soap and I stood behind her, gently massaging her neck and shoulders as I worked my fingers over her tense muscles.

"Mmm, that feels good," she hummed in approval.

I ran my hands slowly down her back and reached forward to cup her soapy tits, teasing her nipples with my fingers. "How about that?" I murmured into her ear before dragging my tongue along the curve of her neck.

"Mmm, yes…" She arched into my touch, pressing her backside against me.

"And this?" I slid one hand down her side and between her legs, caressing her warm center with my nimble fingers.

"Ahh, yes," she gasped, moving her hips against my hand as I slowly sunk one finger into her. She reached between us, grabbing my erection and sliding her hand up and down my hard length.

"Oh, fuck," I growled through my teeth, trying to keep myself from blowing in her hand before I even had a chance to get inside her.

Nora craned her neck around and I crushed my mouth to hers. Her kiss was hungry, nipping and sucking, and when she bit my bottom lip, I couldn't wait any longer.

"Hold onto the bar, baby," I said, clutching her hips with both hands.

Bending forward slightly, she took hold of the metal shower

bar and braced herself. Slowly I pushed inside, entering her from behind and burying myself deep within her slick heat. I stilled briefly, letting her get accustomed to the fullness before pulling back and plunging further in. When I reached her depths, she moaned loudly and grasped the shower bar even tighter.

Holding her hips firmly in my hands, I continued driving into her. I let out a deep, loud groan when her round backside began smacking against me, pulsating into all the right places, and I knew I wasn't going to last much longer. Everything about her consumed me. I leaned over and cupped one of her breasts in my hand, kneading it eagerly and toying with her nipple as I moved rapidly inside her.

Nora's screams became louder, and I knew that she was close. With one final hard thrust we came together, collapsing under the spray of the hot shower.

chapter fifteen

Nora

The next day we said goodbye to the newlyweds as they took off for their Caribbean honeymoon, wishing them luck and offering tearful goodbyes even though they would only be gone for a few weeks. Jake had offered to drive me back home, so we cleared out of the hotel and loaded our stuff into his truck.

Most of the ride back to Beaufort was spent in comfortable silence. We sat close together, the way we used to, holding hands and listening to the radio. I was anxious to finally talk to him about the decisions I'd made, about wanting a future with him and taking my life back into my own hands. I kept waiting for him to bring up the state of our relationship, but he never did.

When we crossed into Beaufort, I knew I couldn't wait any longer. I had to get it off my chest. I was sick and tired of all the uncertainty hanging over our heads.

"Jake, I made some important decisions before I got to Charleston," I began, shifting to face him. "I wanted to tell you right away, but you said that you didn't want to talk about it, so I waited... but I really want you to know now."

"What did you decide?" he asked, meeting my gaze briefly before turning his eyes back on the road.

"I'm done bending to my father's will and letting him control my life. You were right. I've been putting my own dreams aside for far too long. It's time to change that. From now on I'm taking control of my life."

Jake remained silent, so I took a deep breath and kept going. "I'm going to New York to pack up the stuff in my apartment and talk to my faculty advisors at law school, and then I'm coming back here. And I'm staying here. With you."

"Are you sure that's what you want?" He turned to me slightly, but his expression was unreadable.

"Yes, I'm sure." This wasn't exactly the reaction I'd been expecting. I thought he would be happy, thrilled even, but instead, he just seemed skeptical.

"What does your dad think about this?"

I frowned slightly. "Well, I haven't told him yet, but it doesn't matter what he thinks."

Doubt appeared on Jake's face, and I understood why he seemed so apprehensive about my news. He didn't believe that I was actually going to go through with it. My heart sunk a little bit.

"Of course it matters," he persisted. "You need to talk to him, Nora. I need you to be sure, or you'll only resent me later. I don't want to hold you back from anything."

I took a minute to process what he was saying. It made sense, in a way, but it wasn't what I wanted to hear. When I thought too much, about it my doubts had a way of creeping in. As much as I loved how considerate Jake was being, there was a part of me that needed him to give me that extra push when I began to question myself.

We pulled into my parents' driveway and Jake stopped the truck, turning to me and taking my hand in his.

"It's a big decision, Nora, and I don't want it to be about me, or what you think I want. It needs to be about you. It's what *you* want." His jaw clenched, like he was fighting an internal battle with himself. "Go to New York, and if you decide to come back, then I will be here waiting for you. And if you decide not to come back, then it's okay. I'll be okay. You don't even need to explain anything. I'll understand. I just want what's best for you. That's all I've ever wanted."

He was giving me an easy out. But what I really wanted, what I needed, was for him to beg me to stay and tell me that he couldn't live without me. I wanted him to say all the things that I was too scared to say out loud.

Meeting his gaze, I cleared my throat and did my best to sound confident. "I'll see you in a few days. A week at the most. I promise."

Jake ran his thumb along my cheek, his eyes locked on my face in an adoring gaze, as though he was memorizing my features. When he finally met my lips, his kiss was slow and loving, yet somehow full of pain.

I got out of the truck and stood in the driveway as I watched him pull away, wondering why it felt like we'd just said our final goodbye. Nothing about this had gone the way I thought it would.

Had he changed his mind? I thought back to the wedding and how he hadn't wanted to talk about anything and just wanted us to enjoy ourselves. At the time I thought he was trying to make it easier for me, but maybe that was his way of saying goodbye. He may not have put his feelings into words, but I'd seen it in his eyes, felt it in his touch. I hadn't imagined that, had I?

When I climbed the front porch steps, I saw my dad sitting in one of the rocking chairs in the corner and wondered how long he'd been there. As I approached him, he patted the chair next to him, urging me to sit down. My mother had certainly told him about our visit to see my grandmother, so he had to have known that I needed to speak with him. I took a seat next to him and waited for him to talk, or lecture, or whatever he was planning to do to sway me.

"Talk to me, Nora Jane," he finally said. "What's on your mind?"

I was thrown by the fact that he was letting me start, and when he called me by his pet name for me, I immediately softened. He hadn't called me that since I was a little girl, and I couldn't help but recall those days when we were so close and everything in life seemed so much simpler. Looking at him now, I noticed the grey in his hair and the wrinkles on his forehead, and wondered where all the time had gone.

"How come you never told me about the piano?" I asked, unsure of where to begin.

He sighed. "I think it was mainly because it was a part of a distant past that I hardly recognize anymore. My life has completely changed since then, and I'm not the same person I was before. But also, a big part of it was because for a long time, it was painful for me to talk about. I missed it. Playing the piano was a huge part of my life, and I truly loved it. It made me feel whole. I missed it. But I had decided it was best for me to pursue law instead, so I turned my back on music completely."

"Do you ever regret it?"

He let out a long breath. "If I hadn't given up the piano, I never would have met your mother and we never would have had you, so I don't regret it for a second. I enjoy practicing law, and I feel like I ended up where I was meant to be. So no, I don't regret it, but that doesn't mean I don't miss music sometimes."

I slumped back in my chair, more confused than ever. His honesty was unexpected, and it left me clouded with insecurity. Would I regret turning my back on music, or would it lead me to the future I was meant to have, like it did for my father?

"That's the reason I pushed you so hard to follow in my footsteps," he explained. "I thought that, because it had ended up being the right thing for me, it would be the right thing for you too. I let myself believe that I was doing the right thing for you, but I was wrong. We all have to choose our own path. No one can do that for us."

"How do I know what's right for me?"

"There's no way to know for sure what's right. Sometimes

you just have to take a leap, follow your gut and listen to your heart. Somewhere deep down, you know. Just make sure you do it for yourself, and not for me or anyone else. This is about what you want."

"That's exactly what Jake said, too."

"He did, did he?" My dad chuckled. "Well, I guess that's more proof that I was wrong about the kid."

More proof? What he mean when he said he was wrong about him? Never in a million years did I ever think my dad would admit he was wrong about anything. Especially not Jake Harris.

My dad reached out and took my hands in his, the same way he had ever since I was a little girl any time I needed comforting. "It wasn't right of me to do what I did," he admitted. "But I was only trying to protect you. That's no excuse, I know that, but he was a punk kid back then, and you were my baby girl. I thought I was doing what was best for you."

"You may not like Jake, but he's not who you think he is. He's worked hard to change his life around. He isn't a punk kid any-more!"

"I know, I see that now. Obviously I was biased against him, and I didn't let myself see beyond what he was as a teenager. He has changed, and I think he has the opportunity to really make something of himself. I was wrong about him. I'm sorry it took me so long."

He pulled me in for a long hug, and I breathed in the scent of the musky cologne that he'd been wearing for as long as I could remember. I couldn't believe how far we'd come in just one con-versation, and it left me with a lot to think about.

"All I want is for you to be happy, Nora Jane. I will support whatever decision you make, but I only ask that you take your time and be sure of yourself. Whether you decide to stay or come back is up to you, and the people who love you aren't going anywhere. Don't let anyone else dictate your decisions. Trust your own in-stincts."

If only it were that simple.

Jake

I was an idiot.

Two weeks had passed since Nora hopped out of my truck and ran off to New York, and I still hadn't heard from her. Of course, I had practically run her out of town myself with all that bullshit about, *"I'll be okay if you decide to never come back,"* and, *"You don't even need to explain anything to me."*

I'd given her an easy out, and she'd taken it. I should have told her that I loved her when I had the chance. I should have told her that she was everything to me and my life would be miserable if she wasn't in it.

Why the hell didn't I tell her how I really felt?

"Because you're a fucking idiot," I grumbled to myself in response, kicking my toolbox with the toe of my boot in frustration.

I promised myself that I would give Nora space to make her decision, so I'd been trying to stay busy. After the first week passed without hearing anything from her, I'd been in desperate need of a distraction, something to keep my mind occupied, so I decided to build a small shed at the fishing cabin. It was nothing special, but we could use it for storage, and it had given me something to do while I cursed myself for my own stupidity. Most importantly, it required a whole lot of pounding nails with a hammer, so I could get my anger out without destroying anything.

I was lining up a new board on the shed when the sound of a car door slamming caught my attention. Putting the board down, I sauntered around the corner to see who it was. I hadn't heard a car pull in, so I knew it wasn't my dad because his truck was loud enough to hear him coming from a mile away. For a split second, I thought it might be Nora and my heart practically skipped a beat, coming back to life inside my chest for the first time since she'd been gone.

My brief hopes were dashed when my eyes fell on the silver Mercedes in the driveway. My disappointment quickly turned to confusion when I saw that, standing in front of it, was the last person on earth I ever expected to see there.

"Hello, Jake." Nora's father took a few tentative steps toward me before stopping a few feet away.

"Mr. Montgomery," I nodded, eyeing him skeptically. "What are you doing here?"

"I owe you an apology," he said sincerely. "It's about four years too late, and I know it won't make up for anything that I did, but I truly am sorry. Nora is my little girl, and in my own twisted way, I thought that I was protecting her and doing what was best for her. I was wrong."

I felt like I was in the twilight zone. This man had played the role of the villain in my life for nearly five years, and now he was standing in front of me, offering me an apology and actually acting remorseful about all the pain he'd caused. I was dumbstruck. Nora must have finally gotten through to him. Only an angel like her could trigger this kind of change in someone. Apparently she was his weakness just as much as she was mine.

After a few moments of stunned silence, I finally managed to stammer out a response. "I appreciate the apology, sir." I expected him to turn around and leave after that, but he didn't.

"It took a lot of courage for you to come down to my office and stand up for yourself the way you did, and I respect that. I spoke to my friend Stanley Norton after you told me that you had turned down the job, and he mentioned how impressed he was with you. They were real disappointed that you turned down their offer."

"Are you trying to convince me to change my mind?" I asked him. "Is that why you're here?"

"No," he chuckled. "But when he showed me some of your designs, I understood why they were so impressed with you. You have a real talent, Jake. I have no doubt that you'll do some amazing things. I'm not usually wrong about people, but I can admit that I was way off with you. Nora told me how supportive and understanding you've been, and she would be lucky to end up with you."

"That's real nice of you to say, but I haven't heard anything from her since she left. So, it looks like she might be staying after all."

"I honestly don't know," he replied with a shrug. "She hasn't been very forthcoming about her plans, but I made it clear that I support her no matter what. It's a big decision, but it's something she needs to work out on her own. She's been on the same path for so long that she hasn't given much thought to anything else. Before it was nothing more than a dream, and now it's real, which makes it scary. I'm not sure if she's ready for that."

My heart sunk to the pit of my stomach. I'd hoped he might have some reassuring news for me, but his words were a letdown. I tried to hide my disappointment, but I'm sure it was written all over my face.

"Give her some time, Jake," he said. "I'm sure you'll be hearing from her soon enough."

He began walking toward his car, but then turned around suddenly and gestured toward the cabin. "I'd love to give your name to a few people I know who are starting some projects. I'm sure I'm the last person in the world you'd want any kind of favor from, but based on the drawings I saw and the work you did on this cabin, it's them I'd be doing a favor. Please think about it."

After three weeks, I had finally resigned myself to the fact that Nora wasn't coming back. I'd put the ball in her court, but instead of making a move, she decided to forfeit. Sending her father to see me had probably been her idea of closure: a message to let me know that she wouldn't be coming back to me.

I could feel myself sinking into a deep depression, but I didn't care enough to try and pull myself out of it. Every day after work, I came home, lay down on the couch, and drank beers until I fell asleep. I couldn't sleep in my bed because it still smelled like her and was yet another reminder of what I'd lost. What I'd let slip through my fingers. Again.

When I got home on Friday night, I automatically cracked open a beer, slumped down on the couch and ignored Max when he looked up at me expectantly, waiting for me to take him for a walk. My cell phone chimed, alerting me to a text message from Ethan, who had just gotten back from his honeymoon.

Yo dude, the Landing 2night @ 8:00

I definitely wasn't in the mood for that. I typed a quick response.

Nah not in the mood, sry man

I felt bad for blowing him off, especially since he'd just gotten back, but going out was the last thing I wanted to do. Besides, in my current state I wouldn't be any fun to be around. My phone chimed again.

No fuckin excuses! We r going...See u there.

I sighed, realizing that he wouldn't let me get out of this one no matter what. Ethan knew me well enough to sense when I was in a funk. I got up so I could hop in the shower and then hopefully down a few more beers before having to go out and pretend to be having a good time even though my heart was shattered.

chapter sixteen

Nora

I'd never been so nervous in my entire life.

Even though it wasn't my first experience on the stage, this time felt completely different. I sat down on the stool, positioned the guitar on my lap, and lowered the microphone on the stand in front of me. There was a crowd of people surrounding the stage, but my eyes were fixed on the door at the other side of the bar as I went through the lyrics in my head even though I had them memorized.

The lights around me began to dim, and my stomach clenched when I heard the microphone click on. He still wasn't here.

My eyes drifted across the bar to Susie with a questioning look, but she just shrugged her shoulders in response. It was too late to turn back now. The spotlight came on above me, concealing the crowd in darkness and making it impossible to decipher the faces in the crowd. I knew I couldn't stall anymore. Just as I was about to begin, the door opened and someone stepped inside.

My skin began to tingle and the air became ripe with electricity. All I could make out was a silhouette, but I knew it was Jake. It had to be.

"Hey ya'll," I spoke nervously into the microphone as the crowd around me grew silent. "I've spent the last few weeks trying to make my dreams come true, but there's still one more important thing left for me to do. I'm doing something a little different tonight, because for the first time I want to share with you a song that I wrote. This song has been playing in my head for many years now, and over the last few months, it finally came together."

I cleared my throat and started strumming the opening chords on my guitar. When I reached the first verse, I forgot about the crowd in front of me and sang for the one person who mattered to me most.

Flooded with memories when I cross into town
You're around every corner
And each road I go down

Out of all the places within city limits
You show up in this one and find me in minutes
Fighting for breath when your eyes meet mine
Frozen in place with nowhere to hide

Unsure how to act or where to begin
You're in my favorite old tee shirt with the same crooked grin
Those deep blue eyes that I just can't escape
Bring back all the feelings I could never erase

This time around
We won't make the same mistakes
There's nothing that can come between us
We know just what's at stake

My world without you was lonely and gray
Time passing slowly as I dreamed of your face
As hard as I tried to keep you buried deep down
Some part of me knew we were forever bound

You came back in my life when I least expected
Set my world on fire and reignited my senses
After all this time my heart never forgot
It never gave up no matter how hard I fought

Gave my heart away at seventeen
I hope you never let it go
You fought for me, I'll fight for you
That's all we need to know

This time around
No more running away
My heart is yours forever
Please tell me that you'll stay

This time around
It's just you and me
You're all I ever wanted
And all I'll ever need

I breathed a sigh of relief when the song was finished and blushed as the crowd cheered. The lighting returned to normal, and I slipped off stage, expecting to see Jake there, but he wasn't. My heart began to sink. I'd been so sure that he was there, but maybe it was just wishful thinking. Before I could look around for him, my parents appeared in front of me.

"Oh honey, you were just wonderful!" My mother exclaimed, throwing her arms around me. "That was beautiful. I am so proud of you."

"Did you really like it?" I asked, glancing over at my dad who had yet to say anything.

"You are remarkable, Nora Jane." He had tears in his eyes as he pulled me in close and kissed the top of my head. "Absolutely remarkable. I'm so proud of you, baby girl."

"Thank you, Dad." My own tears were threatening to spill over and I blinked them away. If someone had told me a month ago that I would be sharing this moment with my dad, I never would have believed it. It seemed so surreal. "I promise I won't let you down."

He held me by my shoulders and looked down at me with a firm stare. "You could never let me down, Nora. Never."

"Wait a second… how did you know to come here?" I asked them, puzzled at what they were doing there to begin with. I'd called them earlier to let them know that I was back, but I hadn't told them anything about playing tonight or that I would be here.

"We got a little hint from a friend." My dad nodded to someone behind me and gave my shoulder a quick squeeze before he and my mom walked away.

I spun around, expecting to see Susie or Ethan standing behind me, but there was Jake. Nervous excitement ran through me as I took in the sight of him. All I wanted to do was throw myself into his arms and explain why I hadn't called, but I was frozen in place and completely tongue-tied.

Jake stood in front of me with his hands shoved into the pockets of his blue jeans, his face giving nothing away. For what seemed like an eternity we just stared at each other in silence. Finally, his face broke out into a grin, and his blue eyes lit up.

"Are you just gonna stand there, or you gonna come over here and kiss me?"

Relief flooded through me and I flung myself into his welcoming grasp. His arms encircled my waist, lifting me up as he kissed me. We forgot about the people around us as our lips moved against each other, both of us too wrapped up in each other to care about where we were or who saw us. All that mattered was that we were together again.

Jake

When we finally broke apart from one another, we walked outside of the noisy bar and sat down on a bench where we could talk.

"I'm so sorry that I didn't call," Nora began. "I wanted to, I just …"

"You don't need to apologize," I interrupted. "You're here now and that's all that matters." I brought her hand to my lips and kissed it before twining our fingers together and resting them on my thigh.

"No, I want to explain," she insisted. "My trip to New York didn't exactly go as planned, but it wasn't because I had second thoughts or questioned my feelings for you. There wasn't a single doubt in my mind about you or about my decision to stay here. But, something else happened."

"What happened?"

Her eyes lit up and I could tell she was trying to contain her excitement. "I took a chance," she smiled.

Nora explained to me that while she was in New York, one of her friends had put her in touch with a guy who was in the music industry. He'd offered her a one-time shot to show him some of the songs she'd written, so she'd stayed in town until he had an opening to meet with her. As it turned out, he liked what he heard and gave her a chance to record a few of her songs in the studio. He would bring the recordings to a few of the publishing companies that he worked with, give them a chance to listen to them, and if they were interested they could buy the rights to the songs for one of their artists.

"It's obviously a long shot," Nora said warily. "I doubt anyone will actually buy them. But at least I tried, right?"

"I'm so damn proud of you," I exclaimed, pulling her close. "And if they're smart, they will buy them."

"You think so?"

"Hell yeah, I do."

Nora smiled as she trailed her fingers along the bare skin of my arm, sending heat throughout my entire body. God, I'd missed her.

"Well, I hope so," she continued. "But, if it doesn't work out I could always go back to law school later on. New York isn't the only place you can get a law degree."

"Are you sure this is what you want?" I asked, searching her eyes for any sign of doubt.

"Jake, I've never been so sure of anything." She reached up and held my cheek in her hand. "I can't predict what the future holds, but I know that whatever happens, I'll be with you. If you decide you want to take that job in Louisiana, I'll be right by your side."

"I turned it down," I said. "I never actually intended to take it in the first place, it was more about the experience. There's nothing that could or will ever take me away from you. You're all I want, and now that I finally have you back I'm never letting you go. I love you so much, Nora."

"I love you, too," she replied, gazing back at me with a smile that lit up her whole face.

It felt incredible to finally say those words, and hearing her say them back made my heart feel like it was about to burst inside my chest. Just as I was leaning in to kiss her, a jingling on her wrist caught my attention.

"You finally got my present?" I grinned, running my fingers over the small silver charms that dangled from the bracelet I'd left for her all those years ago.

"Yes. I hope it's okay that I'm wearing it now."

"It's right where it belongs." I traced her smooth skin and pulled her in close for a tender kiss, reveling in her sweet scent and warm touch. By the time we drew apart we were both breathless and eager for more. I stood up from where we were seated on the bench and urged her to follow. "I missed you so damn much. Let's get you back home and into my bed. Now."

Nora and I spent the next few hours losing ourselves in one another. When we finally came up for air, the clock on my nightstand indicated that it was the middle of the night, but for the first time in three weeks, I was wide awake. The moon was high in the sky, casting enough light through the windows for me to make out Nora's delicate features. My arms were wrapped tightly around her, fitting her snugly against my chest, and for the first time in my life, I felt like everything was exactly as it should be.

"What's on your mind?" she whispered, looking up at me. "I can see your wheels spinning a hundred miles an hour."

I swept a stray piece of hair out of her face and gently tucked it behind her ear, brushing my fingers along her face. "Will you stay with me?" I asked, gazing deeply into her beautiful green eyes.

"I already told you that I'm not going anywhere, silly."

"No, I mean stay here. Will you move in here with me?"

"Are you sure?" she asked, pulling back slightly so that her eyes met mine. "It's still kind of soon, right?"

"Baby, I've wanted this for more than four years now. I don't want to ever spend another night without you. Will you think about it?"

"I don't need to think about it, of course I will." She pressed a kiss into my chest. "When you know, you know."

epilogue

Nora

"Omigosh, babe! Turn it up!" I squealed, practically jumping out of my seat.

Jake smiled at me and reached for the dial on the car stereo, turning up the volume. My own hands were too busy shaking with excitement to function properly.

"I can't believe it's actually on the radio," I said in disbelief, resting my head back and closing my eyes as I let the music wash over me. One of the songs I'd written had been picked up by an up-and-coming musician, and now it was playing on radio stations all over the country. I still couldn't believe it.

"I'm so proud of you, baby," Jake said, squeezing my thigh. "This is just the beginning for you. Pretty soon your songs will be everywhere. I know it."

I smiled at his encouraging words. He'd been so supportive of me, and I knew I wouldn't have been able to do it without him. A couple of my songs had been picked up after my first recording session in New York, and since then Jake and I had met up with the producer again in Nashville to record more of the songs I'd written. Now, I spent time everyday working on new songs and for the first time, I actually believed that this was something I could do for the rest of my life.

The best part was that I could write music anywhere. That was especially important since Jake had been hired for the project in Charleston, which started next week. He would be working such long hours that commuting back and forth would be nearly impossible, and we certainly didn't want to spend so much time apart. We quickly decided that the best decision was to stay in Charleston for the duration of the project. My grandmother's house was empty, and she had been more than willing to let us stay there. I would be able to write music while Jake was busy with the project, and we wouldn't have to spend any nights apart. It was perfect.

I would even have one of my best friends there with me. I'd been a little bummed to be away from Susie, but then a couple of days before, I'd gotten a call from my college roommate, Olivia, who told me that she was moving down to Charleston. She had been my rock during our college years and was the best part about my life in New York. I still didn't know why she was picking up and moving all the way down there, since the last I knew she was happily engaged in New York, but I was thrilled that I would have her there. Everything had fallen into place. Sometimes I felt like my life was *too* perfect, and any second I was going to wake up.

Things were going well with my parents. They had mended fences with Jake and were completely supportive of our relationship. It was easy for them to see how much we loved each other and how real it was between us. And once that they had gotten to know Jake – the real Jake – they'd realized how wrong they'd been about him. He had totally won them over. Sure, there was still the occasional awkward moment, but for the most part the past was in the past.

Ever since they heard me sing for Jake that day at the Landing, my parents had been behind me one hundred percent. My dad was no longer pushing me toward law, and while he maintained that there would always be a place for me at the firm if I wanted it, I had a feeling that I wouldn't ever need it. It also helped that one of my younger cousins had decided to study law and hoped to eventually join my dad at the family firm. Now that I was no longer plagued with guilt, I was able to focus on music and finally enjoy what I was doing with my life.

Jake turned his truck off the main road and started down a quiet dirt road, reminding me of what we were doing here. He told me that he needed to show me something but hadn't given me any details and I had no idea what it was about. That boy sure loved his surprises.

"Are you going to tell me where you're taking me?" I asked.

"Nope, but we're almost there."

He stopped at a large clearing and hopped out of the truck. After opening my door and helping me climb down, he grabbed a cardboard tube from the back of his truck. He grabbed my hand and led me out into the middle of the clearing before pulling a roll of blueprints from the tube and handing them to me.

"What's this?" I asked, eying the plans.

"A very important project that I'm hoping to start working on."

"Why are you showing it to me?" I slowly began unrolling the plans, careful not to rip any of the delicate pages.

"Because I can't do it without you," he replied.

I looked down at the house plans and gasped. Taped carefully to the first page was a diamond ring. Speechless, I glanced over at Jake and saw that he was down on one knee in front of me.

"Nora," he began. "I still have a long way to go, but I promise to give you everything that you deserve. I bought this land, and it might take me a while but I'm going to build us a house here. I love you more than anything else in the world and I promise to spend my whole life trying to make you as happy as you make me. Will you marry me?"

"YES!" I shrieked, unable to contain the wide smile that was spreading over my face. "Jake, I would live in a shack in the woods, as long as it was with you. When I'm with you, I already have everything I could ever want. I love you so much."

My hand shook as Jake slid the ring on my finger, and when he stood up, I jumped into his arms. He lifted me up, and I wrapped my legs around his waist, covering his lips with mine as tears of joy poured down my face. Everything that we'd been through, good and bad, had led us to this moment. It hadn't been easy, and I knew there would be times when things got tough, but we would get through it.

I'd wondered before if we were kidding ourselves with the idea that things between us could ever be as good as they were before, and it was true. We couldn't go back to the way things were and it would never be the same as it was.

This time around... it was better.

The End.

**Keep reading for a preview of Olivia's story,
Break Away, available now…**

break away
Ellie Grace

When Olivia Mason catches her fiancé cheating, her life gets turned upside down. With no family and no real place to call home, she heads south for a fresh start in Charleston, South Carolina. Determined to gain her own independence and protect her heart, the last thing she needs is a sexy, tattoo-covered guy to cross her path and test her resolve. Just as she's beginning to put her life back together, she uncovers a piece of her past that shakes up everything.

Dex Porter has his own demons. A former Marine, he's haunted by the past and uses whiskey, women and fighting to drown the pain and guilt that consume him. When Olivia arrives in town, he finds himself drawn to her immediately and is surprised by his desire to get to know her. She's unlike anyone he's ever met but he knows he can't get close to her without exposing the part of himself that he keeps hidden.

As Dex and Olivia strike up a friendship and fight their attraction to one another, they begin to chip away each other's walls and help each other heal. However, the past is never far behind and they soon learn that no matter how fast they run, it will always catch up with them.

prologue

Olivia

For the first time since I'd arrived at the office, I glanced up from the piles of reports and spreadsheets that littered my desk and checked the time. It was already almost noon, and despite the fact that my morning coffee and muffin were practically untouched, it was also time for my lunch break.

It never ceased to amaze me how quickly time went by while performing the menial office tasks that went along with working at an investment firm in New York City. My official job title was "Assistant Analyst," which was really just a fancy term for someone who pushes paper all day and takes care of all the tedious duties that all the higher-ups were too busy and important to do themselves. I'm not sure what I had originally planned to do with my business degree, but being a glorified secretary wasn't exactly what I'd had in mind.

I'd been working at Chambers International for almost a year, since graduating from New York University. Investment banking wasn't something I was particularly interested in, but my fiancé, Steven, was a senior analyst at the company, and his father also happened to be the CEO. Oh, and his grandfather was the company's founder. Needless to say, Steven had planned his whole life around working there and eventually taking it over, so when he suggested how great it would be for us to work together, I eventually agreed. He ended up proposing to me a few days later, leaving me to wonder if he was motivated by love or by the fact that I had finally added myself to the grand equation of his life.

Of course, Steven's office was upstairs with the other big-wigs and executives, so we didn't actually work together or see each other aside from the occasional lunch when his schedule permitted. Not that I minded. I wasn't working at his family's company because I wanted any handouts or special treatment. The truth was, I had taken the job because it was convenient, and I hadn't known what else to do.

I normally ate lunch by myself in the employee cafeteria, but today I decided to call up to Steven's office and find out if he wanted to join me. The phone rang only once before his secretary answered in her usual cheerful tone.

"Good afternoon, Steven Chambers' office. How may I help you?"

"Hi, Lynn, it's Olivia," I said. "Is Steven available by any chance?"

"No, hon, I'm afraid he's not. He went home for the day… said he wasn't feeling very well and thought he might be coming down with the flu."

"Oh, no problem. Thank you, Lynn." I hung up. That was strange; he hadn't mentioned that he was sick, and normally nothing could keep him out of the office. I hoped it wasn't anything too serious.

I made my way down to the first floor, but instead of going to the cafeteria, I decided to go to our apartment to check on Steven, stopping at a bistro along the way to pick up a bowl of his favorite chicken noodle soup. He was always making comments about how "cold" and "distant" I was, and even though he claimed to be joking around, I had the urge to do something nice and prove him wrong.

After greeting the doorman of our building, I stepped into the elevator and made my way up to our apartment on the fifth floor. Steven moved into this exclusive apartment complex when he was first hired full-time at the company. At the time, I was still a junior at NYU and hadn't wanted to move from the cozy, on-campus apartment that I shared with my roommate, Nora. However, after graduation when Nora moved back home to South Carolina and Steven and I got engaged, moving in with him made the most sense.

I still hadn't adjusted to living in such an elegant place and being a part of the glitzy lifestyle that Steven had always known. It was an entirely new world for me, and I would probably never get used to it. The only way of life I'd ever known was penny-pinching to make ends meet, shoebox apartments, and always earning my own keep. I didn't like Steven to pay my way, but he insisted on it. I did my best to reciprocate by always taking care of him—cooking his meals, cleaning the apartment, doing his laundry, ironing his shirts and basically catering to his every need. He seemed to like it that way.

I would have preferred paying rent.

Still, I was grateful to Steven. He'd come into my life and taken care of me when I had no one else. So no matter how much I hated cooking and cleaning, I would always do it for him.

The summer after I graduated high school, and only a month before I was to begin my first year at NYU, my mother died in a car accident. I'd never known my so-called father; he left when I was three, and we never heard from him again. My mom was an only child and lost both of her parents when she was young, so she was all the family I had. We moved around a lot while I was growing up. My mom would relocate to wherever there was work available, and since we were never in one place for an extended period of time, I'd never had any true, lifelong friends who stayed in touch. When I lost my mom, I was all alone.

As devastated as I was when my mom died, I began college in the fall as planned, mainly due to the simple fact that I hadn't had anywhere else to go. I went through the motions of school and classes, but it was all a haze. I'd become completely numb to everything around me. My roommate, Nora, was a big help, but she had her own problems. Within the first couple weeks of school I'd met Steven at the college library. He was a junior at the time and, unlike me, seemed to have his whole life together. He was determined, and always seemed to know the right thing to say. All of a sudden, I wasn't so alone anymore. He took care of me and was there for me when no one else was.

So, I became the person that he needed me to be.

I stepped off the elevator and into the hall that we shared with one other apartment. Letting myself in quietly, I slipped my heels off and set them down next to the door before making my way across the apartment. It was quiet, and I assumed that Steven was either resting in the bedroom or working in his home office. Before I had a chance to check, the bedroom door opened, and he walked out with a towel wrapped around his waist, his normally perfect hair all mussed up.

"Olivia, what are you doing here?" he said, closing the door tightly behind him. "Aren't you supposed to be at work?" A look of panic flashed across his features as he positioned himself between the door and me. His surprise was odd considering that our apartment was only a fifteen-minute walk from the office. It wasn't like I worked across the state and a quick trip home was out of the question.

"I'm on my lunch break," I explained. "Lynn told me that you went home sick and I wanted to check on you. I brought you some soup from that place downtown that you—"

I stopped mid-sentence when I heard the sound of the shower turning on. Before I had a chance to comprehend what was happening, a woman's voice called out from behind the closed bedroom door.

"Stevie! What's taking so long? Get your sexy ass in here so I can lather you up, you dirty, dirty boy..."

The door flung open and out waltzed an attractive brunette holding a towel that did little to hide her nakedness. She stopped in her tracks when she saw me, her cheerful expression morphing into fear. Steven was still standing there like a statue, all the color draining from his face as his eyeballs moved back and forth between me and the whore as though he was desperately searching his brain for some kind of explanation that didn't involve him being an asshole.

"Well, *Stevie*…apparently you have been a dirty boy," I spat out, anger boiling inside me. Was this seriously happening? He could have at least found a more original way to reveal himself as a cheating scumbag. I mean, come on. The whole situation was just so…cliché. I honestly wasn't sure whether I wanted to yell, cry, or laugh out loud. Maybe I really was a frigid bitch after all.

"Fuck, it's not what it looks like," Steven said, fumbling for words. He inched slowly toward me as though I were waving a loaded gun around and threatening to blow them both away.

I scoffed, rolling my eyes in disgust. "Don't be an idiot, Steven. It's exactly what it looks like." Finally moving from the spot where I was standing, I stormed into the bedroom and grabbed a small duffel bag from my closet, haphazardly packing the few things I had that meant enough to take with me. My closet was full of fancy clothes and expensive shoes, but I had no intention of taking any of that stuff with me. Steven had bought it all for me for the various parties and events that we'd attended over the years, and I didn't want anything from him anymore.

"Olivia, I'm so sorry," Steven said, slowly coming up behind me. "I was stupid and I let her seduce me, but I swear to you, it was a one-time mistake, and it meant nothing. You've been so distant lately, and after more than four years together, you still won't let me in. I was frustrated and upset. But it will never, ever happen again. I promise to make it up to you. Please, don't go. I made a mistake. We'll fix it and move on."

"You're seriously going to try and blame me for the fact that you couldn't keep it in your pants?" I asked, clenching my fists at my side. "That's the worst excuse I've ever heard! You are a pitiful excuse for a man, and I can't believe I wasted four years of my life with you. Go to hell!"

There was a flash of anger in his eyes, and I knew I'd struck a nerve. I'd never raised my voice to him like this, and Steven was someone who was used to always getting what he wanted. From everyone.

"Where are you going to go, Olivia?" he sneered. "In case you've forgotten, I'm all you've got!"

I zipped up the duffel bag and stood inches away from his face, glaring at him with narrowed eyes. "As far away from you as possible. I'd rather have no one than be with you."

Throwing my pitiful little bag over my shoulder, I turned and walked out of the room, muttering a sarcastic "good luck" to the woman still cowering in the hallway on my way out. I grabbed my purse, left my engagement ring and cell phone (that Steven paid for) on the counter and walked out the door without looking back.

Maybe I *had* always been a little bit closed off, but it was for good reason. Men were scum! Just look at my so-called father. He had claimed to love my mom and me, but at the first chance he got, he abandoned us. I never wanted to suffer through that kind of pain and heartbreak, which was why I'd chosen someone exactly the opposite of my dad. Steven was supposed to be the safe choice. After growing up in a state of constant change and instability, I had vowed to live my life differently. The reason I'd been so attracted to Steven in the first place was because he was predictable, un-complicated and risk-free. I thought I would always know what was coming with him. Turned out I didn't know him at all.

I kept waiting for the crushing pain to hit me, but it never came. I felt angry, hurt, confused and slightly terrified about what I would do next, but somehow I also felt strangely relieved, like a weight had been lifted.

Unfortunately, I had no idea where the hell I was going or what I was going to do. Steven was right about one thing; I really didn't have anyone else.

chapter one

Olivia

I'd been in the car for almost fifteen hours now. When I first got on the road, I hadn't known where I was going. But after driving southbound for a while, I realized that there was only one place I wanted to go. The last place that had ever felt like home.

Charleston, South Carolina.

I'd never actually lived in South Carolina, but my mom was from Charleston and I'd spent time there with Nora when we were on break from school. There was something about the area that immediately drew me in. I couldn't explain it. Maybe it was because I felt a connection to my mom there, or maybe it was simply because the city was so beautiful, but as soon as I'd arrived there for the first time, I just had this feeling—like it was where I was meant to be. It was comforting and peaceful, and somehow being there put me at ease. Since my mom and I had moved around so much over the years, I'd lived in my fair share of places— Pennsylvania, Ohio, Maryland, Virginia, New York—but none had ever felt like home.

After leaving Steven's apartment, I'd wandered around the city for a while trying to decide what I was going to do. All I had was my purse, a few toiletries and a change of clothes. I didn't even have a cell phone anymore. Eventually, I'd hailed a cab to take me upstate to Scarsdale, where my mom and I had lived before she died.

All our stuff, including the old Honda she owned, was sitting in a storage unit there. I could never bring myself to go through it or throw any of it away, so I'd been paying for the storage until I decided what to do with it. Everything from my old life was in that unit. I hadn't wanted to bring any of it to Steven's—it never seemed right to have it there. I kept those two parts of my life separate. But now that I'd left my "new life" behind, it was all I had.

My old clothes were still there, and even though they were from when I was a teenager, I would have to make do until I could buy new stuff. I had started to sort through one of my mom's boxes, but it was too much. As soon as I opened it, the smell of her perfume hit me, opening a floodgate of memories that crashed into me like a freight train. It was amazing how a scent could transport me back in time and make me recall certain moments with absolute clarity. It brought me back to when I was a little girl, watching my mom as she sat at her vanity and got ready for work, dabbing a small amount of perfume on my wrist and my neck, just the way she did it. It made me feel so grown up.

I'd closed the box after I found what I was looking for. I left most of her stuff behind until I actually had a safe place for it, other than the trunk of the car. The only thing I'd wanted to bring with me was a pair of her earrings. They were beautiful, antique diamond drop earrings that had belonged to my grandmother. No matter how tight money was, my mom would never sell them. They had been special to her, and for some reason, I wanted to have them with me.

After loading up the car and saying a silent prayer that the old hunk of junk would still start, I hit the road, ready for a fresh start.

Once I'd decided on a destination, I drove straight through, making only a few stops along the way for food, bathroom breaks and a quick nap at one of the rest areas. I'd also grabbed a paper and thumbed through the classifieds in search of an apartment near Charleston. I knew that Nora was there and I could probably stay with her, but I wanted to do this without anyone's help or handouts. I never wanted to be dependent on anyone ever again. I needed to know that I could survive on my own.

The only apartment that I could afford was in Folly Beach, just outside Charleston. I called the number and arranged to see it the following morning.

After driving more than four hundred miles on I-95, I was desperate to see anything other than the same two-lane highway lined with trees, advertisements for fireworks and stands offering the area's famous handmade woven baskets. When I finally turned onto the exit for Charleston, I was full of nervous, excited energy. It wasn't long before I arrived in the city and saw the familiar cobblestone streets, live oak trees, and historic antebellum houses. It was still fairly early in the morning and the streets were quiet, not yet bustling with cars and crowds. It was like arriving in another time period, one that was enchanting and perfectly simplistic, a seamless blend of past and present.

I crossed the small bridge into Folly Beach and found the address that the woman had given me on the phone. It was a two-story house that sat on the edge of one of the river inlets. There was a small dock on the water and a hammock under the shade of tree. It was paradise.

As I climbed out of the car and stretched my tired limbs, a woman about my age came down the outside stairs from the top floor apartment. Her brown hair was pulled into a messy ponytail, and she carried a little blonde girl in her arms.

"Hi! You must be Olivia!" she greeted me happily. "I'm Amy, and this is my daughter, Sadie."

"It's so nice to meet you," I said, smiling and shaking her free hand. "Thank you so much for seeing me on such short notice."

"It's no problem at all! We live in the upstairs apartment, so we're here anyway. You're also the first person to inquire who isn't a creepy, middle-aged man," she laughed. "It's just the two of us, so I really wanted it to be a woman downstairs. Ready to take a look around?"

The apartment was perfect. It had a bedroom, a small kitchen and dining area, and a living room with glass doors leading to the backyard and a small patio. The lawn sloped down to the shore of the inlet and had a gorgeous view across the fields of marsh. It seemed too good to be true, and I couldn't believe how lucky I was to have found this place. I could easily see myself there.

I liked Amy and Sadie immediately. Amy was incredibly friendly, laid-back and easy to talk to. She was a single mother raising a four-year old daughter, so I already had an enormous amount of respect for her. I knew firsthand just how hard it was to be a single parent, but it was obvious that she was a great mom. Sadie was sweet and absolutely adorable. It seemed impossible not to smile around her. Although the two apartments in the house were separate, it would be nice to be around Amy and Sadie, and I hoped that I would get to know them better.

The downstairs apartment was empty, so thankfully I could move in right away. I signed the lease and wrote Amy a check, eager to get settled in. She helped me unload the few bags that I had with me, and after telling me to stop by for a glass of wine sometime, she left me to unpack my things and adjust to my new home.

I stared down my opponent, taking time to study him carefully and form a plan of attack. We stood across from each other inside a circle drawn in chalk on the cold cement of the basement floor, surrounded by dozens of people shouting last minute bets before the fight started. The air was musty, tinged with sweat, and buzzing with adrenaline, but I blocked everything out and zeroed in on the man who would try to beat the shit out of me as soon as the bell rang. He had a deadly expression on his face, but he couldn't intimidate me. I had already won the fight; he just didn't know it yet.

My lips curled up into a smile. He would find out soon.

"What are you smiling at, you fucking pussy?" he goaded. "You're not even a Marine anymore. You ain't shit, Porter. I almost feel bad that they put me up against your sorry, has-been, disabled, ex-Marine ass."

My smile only got wider. I couldn't wait to teach this prick a lesson. There was no such thing as an "ex-Marine." Once a Marine, always a Marine. The fact that I was no longer considered "fit" for active duty didn't change that. It pissed me off that pieces of shit like him didn't understand that. If it weren't for the partial hearing loss in my left ear, or "acoustic trauma" as the doctors referred to it, I would still be overseas with the rest of my unit. Everything in me wanted to be out there fighting for my country alongside them. But I was stuck here, honorably discharged and forced to retire before the age of thirty.

My body still hummed with the energy and lethal power of a Marine. My brain still functioned and strategized like a Marine. The only way to take the edge off was by beating the shit out of other guys, which is why I participated in "underground" fighting. It was strictly other guys in the military – some who had been discharged for whatever reason, and others who weren't on active duty – but never any outsiders. Outsiders couldn't be trusted, and keeping it secret was crucial because any active military would be kicked out immediately if they were caught fighting. Sure, there was a lot of shit talking and rivalries between the different branches of the armed forces, but there was also a bond of trust. We were all warriors. Fighters.

We got together every couple of weeks and some people fought while others would just watch and place bets. In the end, we were all looking for the same thing: a way to take the edge off so we could function in our "normal" lives. No one ever got seriously injured. There was always someone assigned to monitor the fight and ensure that it didn't get out of hand. There was an element of structure to the whole thing that set it apart from the average bar fight and kicked the intensity up a notch or two.

Reece—the guy who was in charge and organized all the fights—would send out a mass text message when there was an upcoming fight to let us know where and when to show up. With both the Parris Island Military Base and the Citadel nearby, there was never a shortage of fighters or spectators. The locations rotated between different basements, garages and warehouses in the area, usually every couple of weeks or so. Reece took bets on the winners, and it was crazy how much money people were willing to throw down for one fight. I wasn't in it for the cash, but it sure as hell didn't hurt that I made a nice chunk of change every time I won. Which was often.

As barbaric as the whole thing sounded, it provided an outlet for those who needed it and was done in a controlled environment that made it safer for everyone. Before I found this group, the rage was practically eating me alive, and I was picking fights with random strangers in order to get my frustration out. It was better for everyone if my opponents were willing volunteers. Not to mention, it made for a much better fight when I was going up against someone who had the same kind of training that I did.

It was also one hell of a rush.

Some people had counseling or medication, but I had this. This was my fucking therapy. My momentary dose of freedom. The relief was fleeting, and I wasn't stupid enough to believe it was a cure, but it was all I had.

The bell rang, signaling the start of the fight. I watched as my opponent lunged forward, wasting no time before coming at me full force.

That was his first mistake.

I never struck first. Instead, I watched and analyzed my opponent. I examined their technique and looked for their weaknesses. Then, I waited for them to tire, and I used those weaknesses against them. I fought smart and efficiently because that's what I'd been trained to do. I let them think that they had the advantage, and then I took them down.

My opponent landed a few decent punches. A pair of body shots to my ribs and a hard right hook to my face that split the skin and started bleeding. He was strong, there was no doubt about that, but he was already running out of energy.

His breathing got heavier, and I went in for the kill. As he came at me with another hit to the side of my head, I ducked, throwing him off balance and making him stumble slightly. Before he could completely regain his balance, I had already landed a solid blow to his side and an uppercut to his jaw that sent him tumbling backwards. He flung a sluggish punch that I dodged easily and countered with a powerful shot to his ribs.

The fight was as good as over.

I threw a vicious right hook that landed on his cheek and propelled him into the crowd before he dropped to the floor, not moving. The ref slammed the ground three times, declaring a knockout, and half the crowd began to cheer while the other half groaned.

"That's the match, folks!" Reece yelled over the megaphone. "Your winner, and still undefeated champ, is Dex Porter!" He raised my arm above my head and slapped a pile of cash in my other hand.

Piece of cake.

acknowledgements

To the readers: I cannot thank you enough for taking the time to sit down and read my book. With so many amazing books out there to choose from, I truly appreciate you giving mine a chance. I started writing because it's something I love to do, but I had zero expectations. I never would have imagined that so many people would actually read my words, and I am forever grateful!

A huge thank you to Autumn Hull and Andrea Thompson of Wordsmith Publicity, for all their wonderful advice and guidance along the way. Autumn was the first person to ever read this book, and her enthusiasm gave me the confidence to move forward with it.

Tawdra Kandle and Stacey Blake, for all their hard work with the editing and formatting. They fit me into their busy schedules and really went the extra mile to help make this book better.

Julie Parker, for agreeing to let me use her amazing photo for the cover. I fell in love with it the moment I saw it, and I can't imagine a more perfect image for this story.

To all the bloggers out there who signed on to my blog tours, and took time to read and spread the word about my books, thank you!

Last but certainly not least, my family, who have always supported me and been there for me no matter what. Especially Will, who is my biggest cheerleader, even when it means being neglected because I'm busy trying to write.

about the author

Ellie is a reader, writer and overall book lover. When a story popped into her head that she couldn't seem to shake, she decided to pursue her childhood dream of becoming a writer, and released her debut novel *This Time Around*. Now, she spends much of her time dreaming up new characters and stories to write, or curled up with her Kindle reading books by her many, many favorite authors.

To connect with Ellie:
Facebook: Ellie Grace Books
Twitter: @elliegracebooks
Website/Blog: www.elliegracebooks.com

Also by Ellie Grace:
Break Away

www.ingramcontent.com/pod-product-compliance
Lightning Source LLC
Chambersburg PA
CBHW051501170626
46811CB00002B/580